THE ROPE
ARTIST

FUMINORI NAKAMURA

Translated from the Japanese by SAM BETT

**SOHO
CRIME**

The novel was first serialized in Shosetsu TRIPPER
(Asahi Shimbun Publications Inc.) in 2015 Summer, 2015 Winter,
2016 Summer, 2016 Winter, and 2017 Summer through 2018 Fall.

First published in English by Soho Press, Inc.
227 W 17th Street
New York, NY 10011

Library of Congress Cataloging-in-Publication Data

Names: Nakamura, Fuminori, author. | Bett, Sam, translator.
Title: The rope artist / Fuminori Nakamura ; translated from the
Japanese by Sam Bett. | Other titles: Sono saki no michi ni kieru English
Description: New York, NY : Soho Crime, [2023]
Identifiers: LCCN 2022022925

ISBN 978-1-64129-569-7
eISBN 978-1-64129-326-6

Subjects: LCGFT: Detective and mystery fiction. | Novels.
Classification: LCC PL873.5.A339 S6613 2023
DDC 895.63'6—dc23/eng/20220513
LC record available at https://lccn.loc.gov/2022022925

Painting by Utagawa Hiroshige
Rope art: © Moon T/Shutterstock

Printed in the United States of America

10 9 8 7 6 5 4 3 2 1

To all the nothingness.

Part I

1

When I was a kid, I got sucked into a tiny whirlpool.

The waves were not especially high. Something heavy pulled me down, then my feet lost touch with the bottom and I went under, sinking into the abyss. Swallowing my juvenile body, the whirlpool did the only thing that it knew how to do: spin downward.

It hit me that this whirlpool was a part of a gigantic ocean, as obvious as that may sound. Appearing out of nowhere, it swallowed me like it had stuffed me in a bag. Water rushed into my throat, ignoring my attempts to cough it out. I felt the whirlpool passing through my body, but a kind stranger scooped me up. My face broke through the surface of the water.

"Whirlpool," I told this strange adult, but all he did was shake his head. You'd think he thought I had pretended I was drowning. A neglected child, oblivious to all the trouble he might cause, trying to capture the attention of any adult who would listen. To a grown man, the water was embarrassingly shallow. The arm that he had hooked around me was suntanned, two big moles in a row on the part of his skin just under my nose.

She vanished, I thought. When I was being sucked down by the whirlpool, in the middle of it all, I could have sworn I saw the figure of a woman. But no, it must have been some kind of fantasy, washing over me. A woman in the middle of the water, bobbing in the waves. A woman swatting her bony fingers at the waves that threatened to tear off her bathing suit like countless hands. She had to. Otherwise, her body would be seen by all these people. Her long black hair fanned out and undulated in the water. Through the blueness of the moving sea, her body was a distant flash of white. But it had vanished. Had I really seen her? I began to have my doubts. In the kind arms of the stranger, I was pulled out of the water to the safety of the beach.

My head was spinning. Colorful food carts selling ice cream and soft drinks lined the beach. Watery blue and pink, in harmony with the colors of the ocean and the sky. Little by little, though, the palette of the landscape fell out of balance. It was like the sky itself had sighed at me. As if to say, *You had to show up, didn't you?* As if to say, *We were in perfect harmony. Then you showed up.*

THE INVESTIGATORS CRAWLED across the carpet on their hands and knees. The one tasked with capturing pictures flashed his camera. It made a glaring burst of light; the afterimage lingered on my retinae like a bruise. A mass of red, purple and blue, floating persistently before my eyes.

"What's wrong?" Ichioka asked. "This can't be your first dead body."

I had spaced out. His tone contained an air of ridicule. But I had a way of smiling at this sort of thing.

"Sorry about that," I said, trying to come up with an excuse. "I'm still drunk after last night."

My head ached. Again the camera flashed. I wished I could escape the repeated bursts of light.

What made me think about the woman and the whirlpool? I suppose I could have thought about it voluntarily. Every few years, I seemed compelled to recollect what I had seen that day, as if the memory eclipsed my consciousness. Last year, for instance, that night I stepped out for some cigarettes. At the edge of my vision, I felt a shadow darker than the rest. When I asked myself what it could be, my thoughts turned to the woman and the whirlpool. I moved in the direction of the shadow, but it was nothing, just a bar closed down for the night, no light behind the sign. It was well into fall, but a cicada clung to the telephone pole beside the sign, bent on drawing out a sap the concrete pole could never give.

Again, the flash. My heart sped up. No, it had been

racing this whole time. Since the moment I had stepped into the room.

"We've seen a crime like this before."

Ichioka looked at me again. The stubborn afterimage covered nearly half his face.

"The door was unlocked when we got here, but it doesn't look like somebody broke in . . . It's a little aggravating that his cell phone's gone, but we found a couple of business cards inside his planner."

"Right." Was my voice shaking? "I saw that."

The victim was a man by the name of Kazunari Yoshikawa. This was apparently his residence. The way we found the body, his knees were bent into a deep V, tucked underneath him. It had begun to smell offensive, so they carted it away. Above a section of the carpet where three dents, left by something heavy, formed a triangle, two insects flew in circles around each other.

Maiko's card was one of the few objects in the planner. My Maiko? Why did this man have her card? But there were other signs. The shirts and jeans hanging on the balcony. The excessive use of clothespins, bordering on neurotic. The peculiar way in which the socks stuffed on the storage shelf weren't folded one over the other, at the ankles, but were tied in knots, like pretzels. There was vanilla yogurt in the fridge, caramel Häagen-Dazs in the freezer. Chamomile tea beside the thermo pot. All of her favorite things. Even the J-pop CDs that she used to listen to. Had Maiko been living in this place, with this guy? Is this where she had gone when she left me? But what about the body? This was too—

Through the bruised colors of the afterimage, I saw a bed. Small enough two people would be sticking to each other if they shared it. Maiko and that man. That dead man, on that tiny bed, crawling over Maiko's body. My heart sped up again. I saw a tiny black line in the corner of the room.

"Did you check over here?" I asked the nearest investigator.

"We'll go over it again later. See something?"

"No."

It was an eyelash. Blackened with mascara. There were no women in our party, so it had to be from someone who'd been living here. One of the investigators must have picked it up with his shoe cover and unknowingly left it in the corner. It could have been me. That black line looked like a slash mark, like a crack left in the scenery. A hole torn in the fabric of my life. My chest was thumping. As my fingers neared the eyelash, they shook uncontrollably. The second that I picked it up, I felt a strange sensation in my fingertips, through my gloves. Like I was making contact with an abstract notion, something you're normally unable to touch. As I lifted this crack from the floor, my pinched fingers traveled hesitantly toward my pocket. What the hell was I trying to do? It made no sense to hide a piece of evidence like this, when they'd already discovered loads of hair and fingerprints. Hide? Hide what? I put the eyelash in my pocket. What was I doing?

"Hey."

I heard a voice behind me. But no. No one was there. It was Ichioka's voice, though. Yelling at somebody in the next room. Maybe someone had flashed the camera in his eyes. I took my hand out of my pocket. Holding my cigarettes. As if to show someone that I had just been reaching for my cigarettes this entire time. I left the room, stepping on scattered weeklies and conservative magazines.

"Togashi—oh, time for a smoke?"

"Oh, no."

"It's fine, we're almost done."

I headed for the hallway. This was bad, I thought. Why couldn't she have left it looking like a break-in, or a robbery? Left a window or a door ajar . . .

Again a flash of light. I was back inside the whirlpool. What was I thinking? I was tired. I had to remember where I was. The residence of a victim. And like some slacker detective, I was ducking out to have a cigarette. Back to reality.

Once I was out front, I saw Hayama. Squinty eyes. He was standing outside the fence of the apartment building, having a cigarette.

". . . Hi there."

Smoking with Hayama made me depressed. But it was too late. He had seen the pack of cigarettes in my hand.

"Sounds like the director of the first division paid us a visit," I said. "But Ichioka told him that we had it covered."

Hayama gave me a blank look. Blinking periodically.

"He said it was a simple enough case to handle on our own."

Up until that point I had been smiling, but I realized this was not something to smile about. My whole body went tense.

Were the rumors true? They say that several years ago, when a female nurse was murdered, Hayama had declined to book the suspect, in spite of overwhelming evidence, and let him get away, just so he could push him to the brink of insanity. The man turned himself in, but Hayama told him to go home. He refused to acknowledge his confession, so that he could summon him repeatedly and force the man to tell him the cruel details of his murder of the nurse. The crime had been suspended in midair. Why didn't the man surrender himself to some other officer, like at the nearest police station? Was it true the man had hanged himself?

I caught Hayama's line of sight. My fingers were shaking. They were my own hands, but he had noticed they were shaking before I did. Even so, Hayama said nothing about it. People say he used to belong to the first division. The only person that he cared about was himself.

". . . I guess a couple had been living there together. Wonder for how long."

I was trying to smooth things over, but he just squinted and stared.

"The man was probably there a while," he finally said. "But the woman moved in recently."

". . . Is that so?"

"All the girly stuff in there is new . . . Check out the carpet underneath the furniture . . . The marks underneath the stuff that looks like it was his are deeper . . . You can tell that stuff's been moved around."

Trash was scattered in the park in front of the apartment building. As if there had been some kind of a festival the night before. But my life had no room for festivals. The debris only got deeper, one day to the next.

Hayama scanned the park and walked over to his car. His suit was understated, but it looked expensive, classy. Thing is, though, he didn't make it seem like he appreciated a good suit. More like the suit was weighing him down.

Ichioka came out of the apartment. Maybe he'd been waiting for Hayama to leave.

Was it really the same Maiko? I couldn't believe it. This case was way too cut and dry. Like nearly all the cases inundating our society. I had an awful headache, the kind that clamps down on your temples. She's such an idiot. But who was worse? Maiko, or me, for thinking I was cut out to be a detective?

2

The corner by Maiko's place was dark.

According to the real estate office, she was still here.
Which meant she hadn't moved in with him after all.

I thought over the contents of our debriefing.

Kazunari Yoshikawa had been murdered two days prior,
on the fourth of October, and died somewhere between
nine and eleven in the evening. Cause of death was a con-
tusion, brought about by being struck in the head with a
blunt instrument. His thighs were marked with old scars,
unrelated to his death. Judging from the state of the brain
damage, he hadn't died immediately, but remained conscious for some time. The specific nature of the weapon
was a mystery.

I looked up at the nondescript gray building. I had met
Maiko at a club that I visited on a whim and had seen
her there a few times before we made plans to meet up
outside of work. At that point, we had kissed. But the first
time I visited her apartment, and tried to touch her, she

turned me down. I went home feeling out of sorts, but the next time that I saw her, she turned me down again, and the time after that. What made me want to keep on seeing her, despite being refused, was that it felt, at least to me, like she was trying to get over something. Maybe something in her past. After turning me down, it was always her that texted me and said we should meet up again, but if I touched her, she refused. Bursting into tears. This had nothing to do with her job at the club. At that point she was taking some time off.

One day I called and realized she had changed her number, but I called it anyway, repeatedly. Not exactly rational behavior. I called the disconnected number like I thought something would happen. Her new number was hidden somewhere in the massive cloud of digits that encompasses the globe. There were countless times I got as far as the entrance of her building but took off without ringing the bell. I was obsessed. I wonder why?

I typed her room number into the keypad. I could feel a hint of sweat between the buttons and my fingertip. This is a search, I told myself, trying to calm down. I'm a detective, and this woman is suspected of a crime. I realized that a smile had crept over my lips.

"Hello?"

The voice was Maiko's. I caught my breath. My memories of the past were getting mixed up with the present.

"It's Togashi . . . How's it going?"

Feeling myself panic, I elaborated.

"It's not what you think. I'm here as part of an investigation. Do you happen to know a guy named Kazunari Yoshikawa?"

". . . What?"

". . . Open up."

After a long silence, she buzzed me in. The automated door began to open. I forced it the rest of the way. As it was opening, I felt as if the door was telling me to go no further, not if I knew what was good for me.

I headed for the elevator. All I had to do was press the button, but I forced it open too. The sluggish opening of the elevator doors felt like yet another sign that I should reconsider. The lights cast skinny shadows on the floor. Up we went. By then, it almost felt like I was being pulled along, without a choice. The air grew thin. I got out of the elevator, walked down the narrow hall and stood in front of Maiko's place. My pulse was speeding up.

Maiko opened the door.

Just out of the shower, she was a little on the tall side, with long hair and big, observant eyes. She's so pretty, I told myself. She was wearing a beige cardigan over a white tank top. Tight purple sweatpants. My eyes wandered to her chest, the smooth lines of her hips and legs. That man and her? It was the wrong time to be thinking about this. That dead man, with her?

". . . Investigation?"

"Remember? I'm a detective."

I grinned, trying to smooth things over, and took my shoes off. I left them beside her sneakers and stepped inside.

It was a tiny studio apartment. The curtains to the balcony were plain. I sat down on the carpet at the low tea table. Maiko sat across from me. Staying as far away from me as possible. The bed was at her back.

She looked at me like she was frightened. Long hair damp. As if unconsciously, she wrapped the cardigan around her body. To hide the softness of her chest. Her legs were thin but sensual, looking curvier because of her tight sweatpants.

"Kazunari Yoshikawa . . . Ring a bell? Anyway, he's dead."

". . . What's happening?" she said in a low voice.

"He had your card. In his planner."

"My card?"

"You know, the cards you used to hand out at the club. You only went by your first name, but it was real . . . I have one of them somewhere."

She touched her skinny fingers to her damp hair. As if struggling to gather her thoughts, but getting nowhere.

"We found a bunch of your favorite things in that guy's room. The way the laundry was folded and hung out to dry was a dead giveaway, though. That's how I knew for sure."

I gave her a long look.

"I'm sure they found your fingerprints all over every-thing."

She gave me this pleading expression. Like she was sad, but also begging for forgiveness. Of course, I thought. When she and I were together, she gave me this sad look all the time. Without her realizing, that look revealed the way she felt inside. It said to me—

". . . Am I being arrested?"

"So it was you."

"Tell me . . . Are you here to arrest me?"

". . . At this point you're just a suspect. One of the leads we picked up from the cards that guy had in his planner. I'm here to ask you a few questions."

Her cardigan was open just enough for me to see the frail whiteness of her neck.

". . . But I think that we can figure something out . . . I really mean it."

She looked surprised. I could tell she was about to open up. I continued.

". . . So what happened?"

Silence fell over the room. Why, I asked myself. Why am I so drawn to her? Why does she have to be so alluring? The pull was even stronger than before. No, I was so attracted to her that it felt like the first time. Her head was heavy. She looked up for a second, but looked down right away. She started to cry.

". . . At first, he was so nice. But then . . ."

Her voice faltered.

"The first time I went over to his place, everything changed."

My eyes were fixed on her.

"I didn't . . . see it coming, but I had told him, multiple times, that we weren't going to do anything, said it with a real serious face, multiple times, before going over . . . But once he had me there, he pounced on me. I was so scared, and tried to fend him off, but . . . he tied me up. When it was over, he was nice again . . . I was still tied up, but he looked at me and laughed, like it was nothing, and told me he was sorry, petting my head . . . He asked me what I liked to eat. I was scared, but I told him, not really thinking anything of it . . . so he left me there, all tied up, and went out to buy me ice cream and a bunch of other stuff . . . He told me to eat it, made me eat it, then assaulted me again . . ."

". . . How exactly?"

". . . What?"

"What did he do to you?"

I knew this was too far. But I couldn't help myself.

"He tied me up, by the wrists, so that I couldn't move, and . . ."

"Be specific."

"He was so . . . rough with me . . . Look at this."

She rolled up the sleeves of her cardigan. Her skin was purplish red. Her wrists were bruised where she had been restrained. A little hesitant, she lifted the hem of her tank top. Patches of red, however subtle, stood out from her skin. He must have beaten her with something. Those marks filled me with envy. I took a deep breath. I had been the one who asked, but I had to change the subject.

". . . How did you kill him?"

"He untied me, but I tried to escape . . . so he tied me up again."

"Yeah."

"Poor thing, he said, like he felt bad for me, as he retied the knots . . . Poor thing, he said, but he was getting real excited . . . I was scared that he was never going to untie me. That's what did it."

"Did what?"

She sniffled. Her fingertips were sopping wet with tears.

"I told him I would do all kinds of things. Things . . . I thought he'd really like. So he untied me, and this time, to win his trust, I started doing chores . . . except he never left the house."

"How long were you there? We saw the girly furniture."

"I guess . . . about two weeks. That's not really that long. But yeah, he did have women's stuff around. He said there used to be another girl like me there . . . but he . . . he was a scary person . . . He was always home, but eventually he had to run some errands, so he went to tie me up again . . . That's when I picked it up."

She lowered her gaze.

"I'm not sure what it was, some kind of statue thing, but it almost felt like it was saying *Look, look, over here* . . . Then I basically blacked out, and when I came to my senses, he was on the floor, and the blood, the blood was everywhere."

Her voice was getting louder.

"It's possible he's still alive, though. And if he's still alive, he might come here and try to get me. Right?"

"He's dead, though. It's okay."

I went in for a hug. The table was scattered with pills. I recognized them. Xanax. Taken for anxiety. Actually, the whole room was a mess. I felt the warmth of her soft body in my arms. Taking pity on her only made me want her even more.

But you—I was about to say, but I held off. I wasn't about to suggest that she had led him on. Or that this was just like her. Or that despite her sorry state, I wanted her as much as he had wanted her. I couldn't tell her that.

"What happened to his phone? Was that you?"

"I was so scared."

"That's going to be an issue. Where is it?"

"It's not his."

"Huh?"

"He was involved in all kinds of shady business, so he used a phone registered in someone else's name."

My heart sped up. This was a promising detail. The cell

phone company had said nobody by the name of Kazunari Yoshikawa was a client. That meant we couldn't subpoena his phone records or the like.

"Pull any other stunts?"

". . . I took his planner. But I didn't know about the one with all the cards."

"So there's two planners then?"

". . . I guess so."

There was nothing written about Maiko in the planner that we found. Just her card. In that case—

"I can help you."

As soon as I had said the words, I saw the fear deep in her eyes. A fear I wanted to destroy.

She looked back at me. Her tired eyes were wet. But I backed off. This was no time to try to hold her, I told myself. If I take her now, I'll wind up the same as that dead guy. All I wanted was—

What was it I wanted, anyway?

I LEFT HER place and booked myself a hotel room. I had been there only a few minutes when a woman came by. Covered in perfume. She was Chinese. I let her into the dark room. It filled with the smell of her perfume. A vulgar fragrance that used sex as a weapon, in a fight against the world. It was a smell I liked.

"I'm with the police . . . You came here on a student

visa to do work like this? Show me your hands," I told her. "Don't bother trying to run. I'll catch you right away . . . If you do what I say, I'll let you go. You're going home next week?"

She said something in Japanese, then something in Chinese, sounding uneasy, but she had no other option, so she pressed her fingers and her palms into the paper that we used for taking fingerprints. On account of the darkness, I could see little more than her silhouette. One of my sources had helped me find the sort of woman that I needed: somebody without a record, who had come in on a student visa and was working as a prostitute temporarily, before returning home. Ideally, a woman who was planning to go home next week.

All I had to do was submit these fingerprints and handprints to the task force, saying they belonged to Maiko, and the trail leading back to her would vanish.

3

We met up at the precinct to review our findings as a team. The lights shone off the whiteboard, round reflections. For some reason, it really bugged me how they overlapped and spread across the board in blurred ellipses.

It was my turn to speak:

Maiko Kirita met Kazunari Yoshikawa at the club she used to work at. But all she did was give him her card. After that, she quit the club and never saw him again. On the day of the incident, she was at home.

Simplistic as it was, my lie failed to pique the interest of anybody on the team.

". . . There's a woman on the lease."

Now it was Tozuka's turn. He was a veteran. Tozuka had already told me this directly. It was all that I had been able to think about. The lights shining off the whiteboard seemed to spread out even further. As if trying to steal my interest and make me lose my train of thought.

"It says her name is Ami Ito. It stands to reason she was living there with Yoshikawa. Here's a picture . . ."

It was a photograph of Yoshikawa and Ito, in a picture frame. This was the woman Yoshikawa lived with before meeting Maiko. Pretty woman, I thought. Shorter than Maiko, but her long black hair was striking.

"Unfortunately . . . her whereabouts are unknown."

Since quitting her job at a local beauty salon, she had vanished without a trace. If they did find this girl, I was in a bit of trouble. Things would be fine so long as they'd cut ties before Yoshikawa met Maiko, but if that wasn't the case, there was a chance she knew that Maiko was involved.

As the investigation team redirected its attention to Ami Ito, my heartbeat gradually sped up. I had a pretty good idea of where to find her. As long as her name was in the cell phone and the planner Maiko lifted from the crime scene.

The investigation into Yoshikawa's associates was not exactly going well. In part because he was a loner, but mostly because in today's world, it's tough to solve a crime without searching a person's phone or their computer.

This guy had no computer. And I had his cell phone.

As far as the police were concerned, they had two leads on Yoshikawa. The first was Ami Ito, his former live-in girlfriend. The second was—

"Care to join, Togashi?" Ichioka asked.

The meeting was over. At today's debriefing, he was the last to speak. His contribution was that one of the cards in Yoshikawa's planner was for a club that he had done a gig at once. This was their only other lead.

I said sure and stood. One of the investigators was walking towards me. He was a young guy, new to the team. Couldn't remember his name. I took the fingerprinting paper from my bag. The fingerprints and handprints I was submitting as Maiko's. Once the lab compared them with the prints found at the crime scene, they would no longer be needed. There was no way they would match. And no one at our precinct would bother plugging useless prints like these into the database or filing them away.

"Here, these are the prints. For what's her name . . . Maiko Kirita."

That's how I passed them off. Pretending that her name wasn't coming to me right away. The mind of a liar is cluttered with unnecessary lies. As if the lies were seeds that broke away from me and germinated, pushing upward through the dirt toward the light of day. Once a lie passed through my lips, it took on a life of its own, which made the lie all the more enticing. The muscles of my arm were tense, if only just a little, from my shoulder to the fingertips holding the paper. There's still time, I told myself, just as he took the sheet from me. It was just another day at the precinct, but I felt out of place. As if every single thing around me, from the chairs and tables to the walls, was watching me. The young guy walked away, with my future in his hands. Skinny shoulders drooping as he went. Now there was no turning back.

My forehead and my neck were damp with sweat. It's strange. When I gave him the sheet, I made a point of telling myself there was still time to turn back. Even though I had no plans of doing so. I suppose, under the circumstances, this was a natural thing to think. The light shining off the whiteboard started bothering me again. I had to look away.

WE PARKED THE car in the lot and proceeded on foot down an alley, deep into the heart of the city. Black men working for the clubs were calling cheerfully to passersby, sweating visibly. Purple and blue neon signs jockeyed for my attention.

"Hayama skipped the meeting so that he could pay another visit to the victim's place," Ichioka told me as we walked along. "Said there was something odd about the placement of the furniture. You know, like the TV, that sort of thing."

". . . The furniture?"

Ichioka never questioned Hayama's reasoning. And neither did I. Hayama never did anything without a reason. Everything he did had some significance.

". . . This is it."

It was a fetish club. Yoshikawa had evidently done a gig here once. A performance where he tied a woman up. He was a rope artist.

We followed a narrow staircase underground. At the bottom was a wooden door, and beyond that, a metal door. Trance music was playing, heavy on the bass. I showed my badge to a man who had wrecked his face with piercings. He called the owner.

Business was slow. Over the tiny stage, a woman hung suspended from a rope that glowed highlighter yellow in the blacklights. Her entire body, face included, was sealed off in a catsuit. By her side, a man dressed in black leather spun her gently.

". . . It's a shame we can't show you the real deal," a man said, coming over. Must be the owner. Slim guy, in his forties. He was smiling.

". . . Real deal?" I heard myself ask.

"Yeah. They're just putting on a show. How she gets tied up next, how she reacts. It's almost all rehearsed . . . to the beat of the music."

"That so," said Ichioka, making small talk. No inkling of interest in his voice.

The owner looked straight at me. Like an orderly in a psych ward who has spotted an escapee.

"Real kinbaku doesn't work this way at all. The rope artist and the woman up there, they're just having fun . . . It's what the people want. But you can do legit stuff for an audience as well, making it so beautiful and brilliant that it's hard to look away."

He led us up a set of stairs into a lofted area, where you could watch the show from overhead. Since we were higher than the speakers on the walls, it was comparatively quiet. There were tables, but nobody one was around.

"Can you confirm this is the man you hired?" asked Ichioka. He showed him a photograph of Yoshikawa beside Ami Ito. His face was sort of blurred, so Ichioka paired it with a photo of the dead body, in which his hair had been cut short, affording a view of Yoshikawa's face clear to his forehead. Perhaps the owner was desensitized because of the sort of establishment he ran, but he didn't startle at the sight of a dead body. Behind his glasses, his thin eyes were absolutely still.

"Yeah, that's him."

If this guy knew Yoshikawa well, he could get me in trouble. But there was nothing I could do to stop the guy from talking. Not with Ichioka there.

"He came in saying that he had experience and asked me for a gig. A show, I mean, where he would tie a woman up. As it so happened, a rigger on the schedule had just fallen through. I asked this Yoshikawa guy to show me his stuff . . . I can't be giving amateurs the stage, obviously. He had pretty decent chops, though. So I hired him to do a short act . . . but only once. Everything was fine, no problems to speak of. I just got the sense he didn't have the touch, is all."

I watched the woman in the catsuit. Her personality had been erased, so that only the contours of her figure remained, as a description of her body. The glowing ropes dug deep into the softness of her flesh, which was enhanced by the tightness of the suit. The rope artist's hands were quick. He twined the ropes around her body like he was drawing on her with his fingers.

"Kinbaku depends on communication between the rope artist and the woman. Not everybody has the touch, but theoretically, the artist senses where the woman wants to be tied up and proceeds accordingly. As long as you're not doing rope torture, which has another set of rules, it shouldn't hurt at all. In a sense, kinbaku is an intense form of embrace . . . But if all the artist wants to do is tie a woman up, she becomes no more than an object and the whole thing loses meaning."

The owner glanced down at the stage. Blue laser lights reflected off his thin eyeglasses.

"The rope artist has to predict where the woman wants to be tied up, or how she thinks she's going to be tied up next, to keep her feeling surprised . . . He has to surprise her, keep her just outside her comfort zone, in a heightened state of arousal. But as soon as this element of surprise ceases to involve her, it turns into an egotistical mess . . . He didn't have the touch you need to make it work. This element is crucial, whether it's the man or the woman doing the tying."

". . . Right," Ichioka said, showing the bare minimum of interest. Just enough to make his contempt apparent. But the owner had his eyes on me. Like a salesman faced with a likely customer. I thought about the marks on Maiko's arms, where she had been tied up. Imagining her gorgeous skin, gingerly restrained by thin ropes, as she hung motionless and watched sadly as a shadowy figure toyed with her. She looked ashamed to find herself this way. But her shame only egged him on. I tried to rid the image from my mind, but it was no use. Hearing that Yoshikawa lacked the necessary touch, I was slightly relieved.

"He said some pretty wacky stuff. Like how the ropes were in charge. He said he wanted to transcend the woman's desire, and his own desire, to satisfy the desires of the hemp . . . Unfortunately, female subs aren't really interested in metaphysical philosophy. What they want is unadulterated love. That's why he wasn't cut out for the job."

". . . Does he have any contacts here?" asked Ichioka, changing the subject.

". . . I couldn't say for sure. He only worked here that one time. Because of his low aptitude, I doubt any of the women linked up with him."

"What about her?"

Ichioka pointed at the photograph of Ami Ito.

"Don't think I've ever seen her before . . . In this line of work, you get to know most of the performers . . . How exactly was Yoshikawa killed?"

"Head wound. Blunt instrument."

"That's too bad," the owner offered curtly. "Rope artist like him, it would have been much better if they finished him off with a rope. A much more fitting end to his career. Blunt instrument. So cruel. What an unglamorous way to go. Guess he was ready for the scrap heap."

"Scrap heap?" I asked him, without thinking. He must have noticed something in my voice, because he looked a little surprised.

"Sure. He's got no talent. Who needs a man like that? From a woman's standpoint, he was trash."

It would be dangerous to let the conversation drift into criminal profiling. I tried to redirect things, but Ichioka, not interested in any more of the owner's opinions, cut things off to make sure he had time to question members of the clientele. As I was heading downstairs after him, however, the owner whispered something to me.

"That detective really hates me, huh? He hates all of us. What is he, too good for sex?"

"I'm sorry. It's nothing personal."

Down on the stage, the woman in the catsuit spun to the rhythm of the music. I could see it now. This was all show. No real surprises.

"On his way home to hug his kids, he probably stops at

a sex club to have some woman who he's never met suck his dick. He's got a massive blind spot, right in front of his libido . . . Wait. Don't tell me. I bet he's the kind of guy who shows up at a club, pretending he could care less where he was, even though he's only there because he's horny, but still does everything he wants to do, including give the women working there a lecture on his way out the door. Convinced he's holier than thou . . . In my opinion, these people should get preferential treatment in the psych ward. If a person tries to blot out each and every sexual impulse, all they do is stoke the flames. A classic case of reaction formation, as they say in psychoanalytic theory. Conservatives like this guy, brandishing the sort of justice that sounds like something from a PTA meeting, are all a bunch of bigots and warmongers . . . The tendency to view sex as taboo only breeds repression, which hurts women and men alike. At the end of the day, repression is a form of violence. I hope for his own sake that he can change his ways, even a little."

Ichioka was an uptight guy, for sure, but I wasn't going to say so. Nor was I able to acknowledge that he had a hard time putting himself in other people's shoes. He was a lifelong bachelor, after all. And yes, he was kind of a bigot, though I'm not sure what this guy was getting at by calling him a warmonger.

The owner acted easygoing, but he seemed genuinely hurt by Ichioka's treatment of him. I smiled. Convinced

I knew what he was going to say next. *You're different, I can tell. The real show is about to begin. Care to have a look? We're eager to establish good relations with the police.* People in the sex industry cultivate connections with specific members of the force. The same way that gangsters curry favor with specific officers. Police work takes place on the edge of darkness.

When the rope was passed between her legs, the woman onstage shuddered. I became curious about her real face, hidden behind the anonymous, tight mask. With each pass of the rope, she squeezed her legs shut, as if scandalized, but it was no use. Down below, a few people were watching her attentively. You could tell from the movements of her chest that her breath had grown chaotic, as if entangled in their gaze. This too was in all likelihood rehearsed.

I asked the owner something that was on my mind. But first I took a deep breath, making sure he didn't notice.

". . . How about this woman?"

I showed him a photo of Maiko. On the off chance she had been involved with multiple rope artists.

"I'm afraid I don't. Although . . ."

He looked closely at the photo of Maiko.

"She does look dangerous."

4

Beyond the rusted gate of the parking lot, I leaned against my car and lit a smoke. The top part of the floodlight on the wall was outfitted with spikes, to ward off pigeons. Dark was settling in.

This was another precinct's jurisdiction, so I had to maintain a low profile. I looked up at the skinny mixed-use building in front of me. Ami Ito worked, or used to, at the sex club on the sixth floor.

But I had my suspicions. What if Yoshikawa had murdered her? He was a brutal guy. It wasn't out of the question.

With that in mind, it was possible to paint a picture in which Ami Ito was the one who murdered Yoshikawa, but killed herself after the fact. As long as there were two dead bodies, and I could make a clean reversal of the perpetrator and the victim, it would be an open and shut case. If she was still alive, though, we would be alright, as long as she knew nothing about Maiko.

I staked this place out for three hours, watching the exit. But I had no idea what to do next. It felt like I was standing there precisely to avoid having to act. The crew of pigeons walking at my feet kept looking at me with their unexpressive eyes.

I had hopped back in the car, resolved to wait another hour, when Ami Ito came out of the building. So she was alive. She looked younger than in the photograph. Her gait was stiff.

She was a bit shorter than Maiko, wearing a blue dress. A blue that felt designed to soothe my heart. But it was not enough to keep my pulse from speeding up. I got out of the car and trailed her. Unsure of what to do, but breaking free. I found her sexually attactive. I thought of her last customer. What had he done to her? Had Yoshikawa tied her up too? I caught myself, realizing I was staring. As if my desire for Maiko was using her as a vehicle. A scraggly branch jutted out over the road. Watching it wobble in the breeze, I felt a part of me go soft. For some reason, I felt a little buzzed. It crossed my mind that I could kill her, if I wanted to. My heart was speeding up, but somehow the palpitations didn't bother me.

She turned left at the corner just ahead, so I turned too. I harbored the delusion that her life was in my hands. I imagined myself slowly tying up her naked body. Each pass of the rope pulled taut against her skin. My skin was soaked with sweat. She looked at me, eyes mournful and ashamed. I whispered to her. Is this how you like it? Surprised, huh. Should I do it this way? Or do it this way, instead? Gently patting her head, I kissed her, pulling at the rope around her neck. You like that? If they find you dead like this, you know, they'll think you killed yourself.

I smiled, shaking off the fantasy. I didn't have the nerve to do a thing like that. But my pulse showed no sign of slowing down.

Her hand shot up to hail a cab. One stopped for her, and she climbed in. As if escaping from my bumbling lunacy. I tried to memorize the license plate, but the changing traffic light burned through my retinae, hiding several of the numbers in a purple smear. I tried hailing the next taxi that came by, but it was occupied. Some couple. The skeletal driver signaled with his eyes that I was out of luck. Where were they going, where had they been? It was none of my business, but my curiosity about their lives broke through the fog of my insanity. No taxis came by after that.

Given that the address for her workplace was correct, there was a high chance Ami Ito was still living at the address written in the planner. It was unclear whether that was where she lived before or after moving in with Yoshikawa, but the fact that I had seen her out here pointed to the latter. How had he figured out his ex's address? How had it made him feel to write it down? What had he planned to do? I remembered the slapdash nature of the script. A quick notation, just her name, the club's name, the addresses.

This may have been outside my jurisdiction, but I couldn't simply let her go. There had to be some way of justifying asking her if she knew about Maiko, but I couldn't be the one to do it. I would be forced to ask someone for help.

I stepped into a cafe. Before I could do anything, I needed time to prepare. I had only just kicked back a can of coffee, but my body was demanding nicotine and coffee and a break.

The trees outside the window of the cafe were staked down with ties, to prevent them from reaching any further out into the street. Were these trees miserable, dying of thirst? Or maybe they were thankful? Done with light of any kind. As if they'd rather crack in half than keep on standing here. My cell phone hummed.

—*We're in a fix.*

It was Ichioka. His voice was low.

—*There is no Kazunari Yoshikawa.*

". . . Huh?"

My pulse ran wild.

—*The driver's license he had on him lists a place in Miyazaki Prefecture. Ishii went down there to check it out, but he says it's been a parking lot for the past twenty years. Before that, it was a park. So he checked with the municipality, and they said no one matching the description shows up in any of their records. A couple of guys with the same name, but nowhere close to him in age.*

"You're saying . . ."

—His license is a fake. We have no idea who he actually is.

What was happening? I struggled to collect my thoughts.

—The way it stands, it's gonna be a long one . . . They'll probably transfer the case to the first division soon.

My hand holding the phone went limp. He was saying that the first division, from the central office, would be taking over the case. This was a problem. Once the first division was involved, the tricks I'd pulled—

I hung up the phone, hailed a cab, and headed for Ami Ito's address. It hit me that I could have used my car, but it was too late now. Why was I going there, without a clear objective? Logically, there was only one way to check all the boxes: frame Ami Ito and leave her dead, like it was a suicide. That would end things before the first division got involved.

There was no way I could do something like that. But obsessing over something that I knew I couldn't do made me insane. There was only one way to know for sure, and that was to go. I was hysterical. What was happening? I spaced out. Regardless of whether I could actually go through with it, I had to wonder, if I took things one step at a time—

Ami Ito lived in a dilapidated building. I had the taxi let

me off a safe distance away and approached on foot. Not sure why I bothered. Maybe I was in the mood to tell the driver what to do. *This is fine, let me off here.* I had exact change, but for whatever the reason, I pretended I had to hunt for it. Now I was at her building. Feeling capable of anything at all.

My footsteps were so buoyant it was hard to walk. Nobody in sight. As if someone had set the stage just for me. I went around back and found a window. My pulse was wild; it was getting difficult to breathe, but I brushed it off like it was nothing. The back window of the apartment was closed, but it was unlocked.

Just a little peek. Nothing special, a quick look and nothing more. Unless I wanted to climb in the window and wait for her? My heartbeat whipped against my chest. My field of vision narrowed to a point.

I looked inside.

She was lying on the tatami of the bedroom floor.

What the hell? I could have sworn I had just seen her on the street.

I had no clue what this meant, but if she'd killed herself, all the better. If someone else had done it, I just had to make it look like it was her. That would solve things. It felt like there was suddenly another me, watching me breathe. I could do anything. This wasn't anything at all. Besides, I had already stepped way out of bounds. What use was there in being afraid now?

If she was still alive, hanging by a thread, I only had to finish her off.

I felt like I was high. Totally unhinged, I went to the front entrance. Nobody around. Like the other residents collectively decided to stay out of my way. *What's this, a man about to fuck his life up? How fun. I was going to step out, but I think I'll stick around instead.* I was counting on the door being open. I had to worry about fingerprints, though. But wait. I could just twist it open with my fingernails. An ecstatic realization. Of course, look at that, it was a lever, not a knob. My lucky day. Good thing I had let my fingernails grow out! All I had to do was use my nails and twist. I'm so smart. A cool customer. But as my hand reached for the lever, my mind rattled with fear. Opening a door using my nails? What the hell was I doing? I'm a detective. Didn't I have gloves?

I had to make myself calm down. If I was worried about prints, gloves were the solution. I pulled a disposable pair out of my pocket. Fingers trembling. Took a deep breath, looked around. Nobody there. It was open, after all, but the moment that I realized this, I felt a sharp pain, like my heart had been trapped in a fist.

I opened it enough to slip inside and shut the door behind me. Nobody saw. And from here on out, no one could possibly see me. No matter what I did, I was hidden from the world.

What was I supposed to do if she was still alive? To

make it look more like a suicide, I had to . . . wait, hold on, what the fuck was I doing here? Too late. I was in too deep. Let's see the body. Once I had seen it, I would figure something out. A door led from the kitchen to her bedroom. I suppressed my nausea. This was no place to vomit. That was the one thing I could not allow myself to do.

It was a man. Sopping wet long hair and a skinny body. It wasn't Ami Ito after all. Water seeped from the tatami mats of the bedroom out onto the kitchen floor. The beach, I said to myself. The beach where I had nearly drowned as a kid. What now? This was bad. So much for being a cool customer. I better not leave any trace that I was here.

I WALKED DOWN the busy streets and, feeling sick again, puked in the gutter. It occurred to me that I hadn't eaten anything all day. Nothing had gone down my throat except for coffee. I felt besieged by a mysteriously fatal aura. A fortune teller gazed at me as I walked by. The kind that makes their living on the sidewalk, but appears to have evaded their own luck. He made me angry, but I walked closer. He was an old man. For some reason, his eyes reminded me of the unexpressive eyes of the pigeons from earlier.

"What?" I asked.

The old fortuneteller simply stared back at me.

"Do you see something? Huh? What do you see in me?"

The man was frightened. Now what the hell was I doing? I shook my head and apologized. I tried to give him money, but he didn't want to take it. I walked away.

What was that about? I struggled to collect my thoughts. I couldn't kick the image of the beach. Drowning, only to be saved by some strange man, who led me up the shore. A scene of perfect harmony, until I ruined everything.

But there was more to the story. A continuation that I did my best not to recall. To this day, I was unable to comprehend what happened next. I couldn't even tell if it had really happened. The stranger took my hand as we walked up the beach, through a mess of plastic bags from the convenience store. A pair of nail clippers flashed at me from the sand. I saw another man beyond a fence, trying to get to us. Then the man holding my hand spun around and said something to me. A cryptic word that didn't fit the situation. Whispering it in my ear, like he was blowing at an insect.

". . . Murderer."

5

There was a girl there. Cowering and shivering, on account of her wet hair. This was awful. She was just a skinny little thing, looking away from me. I approached her. Somebody had to give her a hug. I put my arm around her shoulder. She latched on to me.

"Don't worry, it's okay . . . What happened here?"

—*I am a figment of your neurosis.*

Her arm squeezed tight around my waist. She was a pretty girl. Lips pursed, eyes fixed on some specific point. A twitching in the muscles of her face. Pretty.

—*I need you to protect me. Don't ever let me go.*

"Okay. I won't," I said, as gently as I could.

—*Don't listen to anything anybody says.*

"I won't."

I held the shivering girl tight. Holding her dearly. She was really shivering.

—*I'll never let you go. Never ever. Don't listen to what anybody says.*

Her voice became a whisper. A secret held between the two of us.

—*Especially not the doctors in the white coats. We'll show them. They don't know anything. Those stupid doctors just gave up on me. See, they said. See! There's just no fixing her.*

I OPENED MY eyes. It felt like I could scream. My pulse so fast it hurt.

The sultry air inside the car was nauseating. I'd been unable to sleep and went straight into the morning briefing, then went out to the precinct parking lot and holed up in my car. Sleep hit me like a sandbag. Ten in the morning. Barely any time had passed. I'd only slept one or two minutes tops.

Thirsty as hell, I got out of the car and went back to the building, where I bought some water from the vending machine. I chugged it down. My heart wouldn't let up. Head pounding, I stepped outside and lit a cigarette.

I thought about the content of the meeting. The search had been reoriented around Ami Ito. As if determining her whereabouts would be enough to solve the case. I couldn't gather my thoughts. What was that body all about? I couldn't let it go. Had Ami Ito killed him? If so, why? Did she just go about her business with a body on the floor?

Either way, it was only a matter of time before they discovered where she lived. Arresting her, they'd find a body in the bedroom. Sufficient reason to convince them she had been the one who murdered Kazunari Yoshikawa. Letting Maiko off the hook.

But I couldn't let that happen. Instead of framing someone for the crime, I'd much rather find a way to leave things messy. People don't realize, but tons of crimes go unsolved all the time.

I needed to make contact with Ami Ito. That was the most pressing task. She and I could work together and make the man she'd killed, or so it seemed, look like he'd killed himself. Then we just had to find some way to paint him as the one responsible for killing Yoshikawa. If we were unable to skillfully manipulate the corpse, I could just let her get away. Don't think for a second that I couldn't pull it off. Things would end without her being arrested for the murder of the dead man, and the Yoshikawa case would be a wash. Everything would work out fine.

A disturbing feeling spiraled through my mind. What was that about? I must have had some kind of dream just now, when I was sleeping. I couldn't remember though.

"Togashi."

I looked up to find Hayama. My heart beat even faster.

"Oh, Hayama. How long have you . . ."

"How long? This whole time."

He eyed my cigarette. Blinking at me. At his wrist, I saw a bracelet of prayer beads. Looked like crystal.

"Sorry . . . I guess I'm, uh, a little behind on sleep."

"Not surprised."

Hayama lit a cigarette. That's odd. I could have sworn he was already smoking. He was in a talkative mood. For whatever reason, he was looking at my feet.

"We gotta find a way to pick up Ami Ito," I said, fishing for an appropriate topic. "It seems like we've almost figured everything out . . . including the reason behind Yoshikawa's alias."

"Nah," Hayama told me with a blank look on his face. "You see the women's clothing at the crime scene?"

My heart did somersaults.

". . . Yeah."

"Not a lot of clothes, for someone living there."

I took a deep breath, but carefully, so that he wouldn't notice, and tried to formulate a counterargument. Maybe she had packed them up when she escaped? But there was no use arguing with him. Persuasion would only make him more suspicious.

". . . Fair point."

Hayama took in my expression. Was I imagining things? What's with the intimidation?

"She must have packed a few things when she left," Hayama said, "but all we found was brand-name clothes . . . which stood out from that place like a sore thumb. Would she leave those behind? I suppose if they were gifts from Yoshikawa, then it's possible, but still."

"Right."

That was the most that I could say. I checked to make sure that my fingers weren't trembling.

"From the looks of it, he picked them out for her to wear when she was over. Did you see Ami Ito?"

Listening to him speak, I took one deep breath after another.

"Her photograph, I mean. Those clothes don't suit her at all. I bet if we did take her into custody, the clothes wouldn't even fit her." Hayama lit a cigarette. Smoke wandered from the tip. "Wrong size."

Yoshikawa had bought those clothes for Maiko, for her to wear during her period of captivity. This detail had been worrying me. But for the time being, Hayama was just guessing.

"What about Maiko Kirita?"

"Huh?"

"Tell me about her. What's she like?"

My heart beat audibly against my chest. I realized I was staring at Hayama, tense all over, but I let it go. What was happening? Why bring up Maiko now?

"Average, I guess. Pretty enough, if she puts on makeup."

I tried to say the sort of thing a man would normally say.

"What was she wearing?"

"Sweats and a beige cardigan . . . house clothes."

"I see."

". . . See what?"

My pulse was off the rails. Could I possibly sound nonchalant here?

"Her card."

"Card?"

"We only got a few prints off the cards, but what we did find doesn't match what showed up in the rest of the room. And her prints didn't show up anywhere. But I noticed something odd about the pattern of the skin oils."

Okay. So they didn't find her fingerprints on her card. That's how I got away with swapping out the fingerprints. But skin oils? What about skin oils?

"Generally, you're going to find skin oils on at least three spots on a card, front and back. Oftentimes, it's four or more. It's good manners, right? You hand someone a card with both hands. And accept it with both hands. Or one hand, maybe, if you're impolite. But that's a card from a nightclub. Maiko would have used both hands for sure. And yet, there's only oil in two spots. At the edges, on the left and right."

I struggled to compose my thoughts.

"Almost like it went from one set of pinched fingers to another. Pretty casual exchange, wouldn't you say, for a hostess club? It's strange."

So . . . Yoshikawa ducked into the club and Maiko slipped him the card with one hand? No way. First off, he wasn't a customer.

"Her alibi is that she was home. Likely story. Then again, the prints from the crime scene don't match, either . . . Whatever. It was just a hunch."

6

Nursing a headache, I waited for Ami Ito to appear.

I'd been staking out the building of the sex club where she worked for over two hours, but there had been no sign of her.

On the website of the business in question, all the faces of the girls were blurred. Rid of their identities, presented only with a caption for their measurements. The hobbies and the favorite things they listed in their profiles were the sort of things that anyone could like. There was no way to tell which one of them was her, much less what hours she worked. And I couldn't exactly stop in for a drink.

Maybe she was off. But I couldn't wait at her apartment. There was the body to consider. Come to think of it, she probably wasn't ever going back.

It was risky, but I decided to go back over there and hunt for clues. Focusing on the places that looked lived-in. Was my judgment sound? Didn't matter, I was almost out of time. The task force was making the investigation public, in the hopes of finding her. I got in the car and drove over to her apartment.

Doing something about Maiko's alibi was crucial, but for the moment this was the priority. If Ami Ito was arrested, I would be in deep trouble.

Though I wasn't doing anything out of the ordinary, my heart beat out of control. I made myself loosen my death grip on the steering wheel. My vision blurred. For an instant, I had blacked out. Wow. I stopped the car on the shoulder of the road and drank some coffee. But all it did was speed my heart up. Was a lack of sleep the only factor here? Perhaps some part of me was trying to thwart my actions. As if keeping me away at all costs, even if I caused an accident and lost my life. At times our inner world blows through the surface of our lives, defying reason. Though maybe I'm just talking like this on account of lack of sleep.

I parked in a back alley, a safe distance from her place. Again, my twitching body asked me for some nicotine and coffee and a break. I lit a cigarette and took a deep haul as I started off, casually looking left and right, to make sure that the coast was clear. The window was unlocked, same as before. I peeked inside and gasped.

How could this be? I went around the front. Looked both ways, pulled on my gloves, and touched the lever of the door. It was unlocked. Quietly, I opened it and slipped inside. Passed through the kitchen, through the door into the bedroom.

The body was gone. Had someone taken it away? But the tatami wasn't damp. My pulse drummed through my chest. My vision narrowed. The body hadn't simply disappeared. Something else was happening here. What the hell was going on?

I heard footsteps and went stiff. Frozen in place. Someone was coming. Were they here? Or next door? My eyes shot to the window. If I hurried, was there time to throw it open and jump out? No. The footsteps came as far as the door to the bedroom and stopped. But why? I found a closet door and shut myself inside. Barely fit. My heartbeat throbbed against my chest. I heard the front door open. Who was it now? I couldn't believe what I had seen just now. My mind ran wild. But next thing I knew, my breathing had calmed down. Something inside of me, but separate from me, smoothed my breaths without a sound. Of course. I couldn't make a sound at any cost. I heard the bedroom door click open. Opening the closet door, just a crack, I tried to see into the room. It wasn't easy. But I caught a piece of a blue uniform. A cop? Had the police already secured the scene? Had Ami Ito been arrested? Why hadn't there been caution tape? Maybe I beat them to it? What if they opened up the closet, though? What was I supposed to do? My mind was doing crazy things. I was useless. Imagine, a detective, being found by the police, hiding like this. I'd probably be carried off with my head spinning. Dizzy, struggling to breathe. Something was spreading through my body. Warmth. Something warm. But why? I had to smile. I couldn't lose it now. Was my head screwed on straight? The pounding in my chest and neck was brutal. I was about to cry. Here? Now? No way. Absolutely not.

But just like that, they left the place. An initial visit, nothing more. What was up? No time to think. They left through the front door. Slowly as I could, I pushed open the closet door. If I was going to run, this was my chance. Stopping near the window, I listened for a moment, to make sure no one was there, then opened it up far enough to slip outside and drop onto the street. The sensation of the sandy ground under my feet made me catch my breath. Shoes. I had left my shoes inside.

My vision narrowed to a pin. What was I doing? Once again, I heard footsteps. More than last time. By the entrance. There was no way I could go back for my shoes. A voice explained something to someone. Was it the super? Talking to the cops? Were the guys I had just seen actually cops? I couldn't get a read on things. My knees went weak. Regardless of what happened, I couldn't go back for my shoes. I had to get away, as quickly as I could.

So I walked down the street in just my socks. Able to walk, despite the weakness of my legs. Definitive proof that I was guilty of trespassing.

NEXT THING I knew, I was in front of the door to Maiko's apartment.

How had I gotten myself here? The world was dark. Had I slept in my car? Was this a dream? It couldn't be. I looked at my feet. Just socks.

Maiko opened the door, looking at me like she was afraid. That look, I said to myself. Afraid and yet somehow seductive at the same time.

I stepped inside. Same as last time, she was wearing a beige cardigan over a white tank top and those purple sweatpants. They clung to her, accentuating the curved lines of her body. I caught my breath. Opened my mouth. Unable to prevent my voice from trembling.

"Do you know a woman by the name of Ami Ito?"

She had that sweet smell, like after a shower. It must have been coming from her hair.

"Don't think so . . ."

I reached out and pulled her in for a hug. She showed me no resistance.

"Sure you do . . . her name was inside Yoshikawa's planner."

"Doesn't ring a bell."

Don't lie, I grumbled to myself, inside my head. She was, though. She was lying. I looked at her face. Big eyes glistening.

Come on. The laundry I had seen at Ami Ito's apartment, left to dry in that peculiar way. Maiko's favorite ice cream, in the trash can. Her favorite CDs on the book-shelf.

I gave her a kiss. Using my tongue. In response to my tongue's fierce gyrations, she touched the tip of hers to mine, just twice. The shampoo smells of her wet hair enveloped me. I touched her breasts. Groping my way along. She grasped my forearms with her fingers, but not so hard that it felt like she was pushing back. She was so soft. I kissed her again. And again, and again. Then I laid her on the bed.

". . . Did Yoshikawa really lock you up?"

Once I had most of her clothes off, I buried my face in the paleness of her breasts and dragged my lips over her nipples.

"Ohh . . ." she said. I held her arms down, try as she might to get away.

You, I thought. *No, not just you. The two of you.*

Why did the two of you kill him?

I touched her vagina through her purple underwear. She was insanely wet. I pulled down her underwear and started fingering her.

"Oh . . . Ohhh."

"You don't really want to fuck me, do you?"

I went deeper with my finger.

"No, it's just . . ."

"Then why are you so wet? Tell me."

She looked at me like she was ashamed. Eyes pleading

me to stop. But at the same time, she was crying out with pleasure, her vagina so wet I could hear it getting wetter. Borderline scary.

"Stop. I can't . . . I can't take it, or I'm gonna . . ."

"Yeah?"

"Stop, I'm gonna, ah, I'm coming, ahh!"

At this point she was flailing, but I held her tight with my left arm, to keep her under me, fingering her even harder.

"Stop, stop."

Closing tight around my finger, she writhed and twitched and bent her back into a deep curve. Her freshly shampooed hair was a mess. Her chest heaved up and down. I kissed her passionately.

At what point did you plan on killing me?

I put my penis inside of her. She was so wet she soaked the bed.

"Ah, ohhh!"

"I love you."

I started thrusting. Her vagina was so wet the bed was drenched. With every thrust it made a sucking sound, like a tongue pulling on the inside of a cheek. She turned her face away from me.

"Why won't you look at me? You hate me that much?"

"No."

"If you hate me, and you're just letting me do this, so that I'll protect you . . . then why are you so . . . ?"

"Stop! I'm—"

Again she screamed and closed her vagina tight around me. But she just kept getting wetter. Almost impossibly so. I had no idea that she could be so incredibly nasty. I turned her head to mine so I could kiss her again. Sinking both hands deep into her wet hair. I didn't care what happened next. I didn't care.

"Oh, no, ahh."

Now she was thrusting. It made it hard to tell how much of the work I was doing.

"Ahh! Ahhh!"

"I love you."

I caught her smiling, only for an instant. What was that? Thrusting hard, I dredged my lips over her neck and closed them tight around her nipples. Her arms locked around my back. It was getting hard to breathe.

"Oh, ahh!"

"Can I finish . . . inside?"

"Yeah, yeah, ahhh!"

The pleasure peaked. I came inside of her. A second and a third time, pumping hard. I was satisfied and spent, but her vagina gripped me like a vise. As if preventing me from pulling out. She made these little twitching movements with her legs, closing around me.

She looked at me with gleaming eyes. Cheeks flushed. Again we kissed.

I gave her a long, steady look. There was no way that I

could let her go. So dear to me. Dearer than anything that I would ever know.

I had to get out of here and fast. But if I wanted to get out of here, I could just leave.

7

Lying in bed, I embraced her. Maiko had her arms wrapped around my neck.

". . . About your alibi."

". . . Huh?"

"You can't just say that you were home . . . you gotta change it."

She gave me a quizzical look and surprised me with a kiss. She was smiling. *You sure you're the same woman who killed that guy?* I almost asked her, but I stopped myself. She lacked the necessary self-awareness.

I thought about the shoes I left at Ami Ito's apartment. On second thought, they weren't so big a problem after all.

I bought them two years back. My shoes wear out like nothing, interviewing suspects, so I bought a bunch of cheapo pairs at the same time. It would be tough to nail me down with just a pair of shoes like that. This type of evidence was as unhelpful as it gets.

It was doubtful that my fingerprints would show up on the shoes. Most people only touch the laces. And even if they did show up, who would think to check the fingerprints of the detectives of another jurisdiction?

Still, I thought. Was that really just an honest mistake on my part? I'd heard somewhere before that human error isn't always accidental. The unconscious mind can take over and intentionally make a mistake, to underscore some aspect of our desire. Or maybe I'm just overthinking things.

"The task force heard your alibi from me. So you can't up and change it right away."

I tried to focus. Right now, especially.

"Basically . . . you'll need another alibi on-hand, to use in case they question you again. And this new alibi has to explain, in logical terms, why you had no choice but to lie the first time, saying you were at home. The sorrier you sound the better. Make it sound like you are only telling them under duress. It'll sound more real that way, harder to refute . . . maybe tell them you're a sex worker. I have some contacts that will probably vouch for you."

". . . Or I could just mention my old club. They still have me on the books."

". . . You weren't involved in sex work there, though, right?"

"The boss was. He had the manager run the club so he could do it on the side . . . One time he covered for a girl who almost got busted for drugs, so I think he's used to it."

She looked at me, seeking approval.

"Can we trust this guy?" I asked.

"He's a professional. I mean, he's hid some girls who were in really deep trouble . . . He hates the cops, so I'm sure that he'd help me out."

She didn't sound particularly worried. Lifting my fingers, she led them down between her legs. We had only finished a few minutes earlier, but her vagina . . .

". . . In that case."

I gave her a kiss. There was no way I could resist her.

"Instead of telling him you did it, say you need an alibi because the police think you did it, for some reason . . . Then I'll stop by, pretending it's a routine investigation. To see if we can trust him."

THOUGH A LITTLE on the old side, the apartment that housed the escort agency was incredibly generic. The front part had been made into a reception area. The living room, dining room and kitchen had been carpeted, a woman sitting on the floor in each, staring down into her phone. Plain women with black hair.

The man who opened the door ushered me into a room out back. It was a simple office. Nothing special about the buildout or decor, but the lights were low, perhaps too low. So was the temperature; the air against my skin was dry.

". . . Maiko Kirita, huh . . . Let's have a look."

Before him was a stack of resumes. He was probably in his fifties, nice features for a ragged face. Maiko had said this was a separate gig for him, but it was possible that he was being forced to do it by the yakuza.

These days, a lot of normal people wind up in this line of work. But this man was in his element. He must have been connected with the industry for a while.

"Oh, you mean Mai-chan . . . she obviously wouldn't use her real name here. What day were you asking about?"

His face may have been ragged, but his performance was anything but sloppy.

"The fourth of October. From nine to eleven at night."

He glanced up at his computer.

". . . Yup, she was here."

"Show me."

He was right. Her name was right there on the screen, along with the totals for the night in question. This guy really was a pro.

"I can't tell you anything more. I don't pry into my women's personal lives."

". . . Where does she meet her clients?"

"That love hotel, right there. Across the way. We have a business relationship."

There were no security cameras in here. Nor would there be any at the love hotel. There was no way to confirm what he was saying.

"How can you be sure that she was there? What if she went someplace else?"

"Not possible. I've gotten all the check-in calls."

"You mean she's checking in with you?"

"No, from the management over there. It's all here in the records. Never once have they complained about her not showing up. . . Will that be all?"

"I want the phone number of the guest she saw that night."

"Give me a break." He laughed at me.

"This is a criminal investigation. If you insist on not cooperating . . ."

"You're putting me in a tough spot . . ."

"Tell me now, and there won't be any trouble."

". . . Here, okay?"

The man showed me his phone. He must have plugged her name into another girl's job. What was he going to do if I questioned this guy? He didn't try to stop me from writing the number down. Or had he taken care of that part too?

Why, though? It wouldn't have taken him much time. But why would he go to the trouble of all this for her?

"What's your relationship to Kirita?"

"Huh? I'm her boss."

"Anything more than that?"

"Our policies are strict here. If I did something like that, I'd lose my neck. The guys on top have no patience for it. See?"

He showed me his right hand. It was missing not the pinky finger, but the middle one.

"Say what you will about this industry, but I'm done making mistakes. Besides . . . she and I don't get along."

Overthinking things again. Or maybe I was simply envious.

I realized that the man was staring at me. Our eyes met, but instead of looking away, he broke into a smile.

". . . You're a nice guy, for a detective."

"Huh?"

"I make my money off these girls. It's a shitty way to make a living. But I don't get the sense you hate me for it."

He raised his eyebrows. I looked back at him, but he wasn't about to flinch. Something in the air had changed.

"I can tell you're not an insensible man . . . am I right? I knew the second you walked in."

"What are you getting at?"

"Want to have some fun?"

It was the same look that I'd gotten from the owner of the fetish club. People in this line of work are eager for a friend who'll tip them off before an unexpected visit. Like I said, a detective's work happens on the edge of darkness.

"I think I'm good today."

". . . There's a girl who'll let you do anything you want."

His posture was already bad, but he leaned in even further.

"I'm not just talking normal kinky stuff. *Literally*

anything you want, except she doesn't work for me. She's simply an acquaintance, who I'd gladly introduce to a friend such as yourself. It won't cost you a thing. This time . . . What do you say?"

He showed me a file that contained a two-page spread on lightweight paper. Anything I wanted? What kind of business was he running? Who was this guy?

Looking at the photograph, I felt my heart speed up. Surrounded by a group of Chinese or Southeast Asian women was a single Japanese one.

Ami Ito.

A coincidence? It couldn't be. When I looked up from the file, he was still smiling at me.

"Who's this?"

"She's a beauty, right? Hard to believe that she'd be on a list like this one."

"Is there something you're not telling me?"

"Me? Course not. I don't make the list myself. They just send it to me."

No way. Was this for real? It couldn't be.

"Looks like you see something you like . . . Let's give her a call, shall we?"

8

The love hotel was not exactly what you'd call hygienic. One of those places where human desires concentrate and condense. I was waiting in the darkness of the designated room when Ami Ito arrived.

She was a bit shorter than Maiko. Black hair. Pretty. She looked much younger than she'd looked in the photograph. But the glare she gave me when she stepped into the room said a lot.

Without saying a word, she started taking off her clothes. I was surprised and tried to stop her but was unable to get the words out. A few practiced motions later, she was completely naked and stepped by me to the bed, where she lay down, facing up. Done looking at me. Blue underwear on the floor.

Is this when I was supposed to do "anything I want," absolutely anything?

Watching her gaze miserably at the ceiling, I realized that I felt aroused.

There I was, about to have my way with a miserable woman. Like she was just an object. A vessel for the darkness inside of me.

I let out a breath. I couldn't stoop that low.

"Sorry . . . I'm not really here for that."

But she just lay there, staring at the ceiling.

". . . Did they tell you who I am?" I asked.

"I have no idea who you are," she said softly. Not moving a muscle.

"I want to talk to you . . . You're Ami Ito, right?"

"No."

"Save it, okay . . . I know who you are."

That made her sit up. Not bothering to cover herself.

"I'm sorry," she said, "but you don't."

I looked at her. I was seriously confused. Like I'd found myself in the wrong room. She didn't look like she was lying.

"I won't do you any harm . . . I'm a friend, okay?"

"Friend?"

"I'm here to help you."

Ami Ito looked at me like I was crazy.

"Why? Who are you?"

"I'm a detective."

Springing up, she ran past me and grabbed her clothes. I grabbed her arm. She tried to stop me, but she failed. I pushed her down onto the bed.

"Hold up. I'm not trying to arrest you."

". . . What is this?"

"I can help you cover up the murder you committed. Where's the body?"

". . . Huh?"

"The dead body."

". . . What are you talking about?"

I looked at her, unsure about this now. She really didn't look like she was lying.

". . . Are you sure that you're not Ami Ito?"

"Absolutely sure."

"You do work at INCONSCIENT, right? The sex club."

". . . Yes."

"What about Kazunari Yoshikawa?"

"Who?"

It was an alias, after all. Maybe she knew him by a different name? I wished I had a photograph.

"Am I correct that this is your address?"

I showed her the address in the planner. She shook her head. What now? This made no sense.

Kazunari Yoshikawa's planner mentioned Ami Ito. How was it that the address for her place of work was right, but her home address was wrong?

"Show me your license. Some kind of an ID."

"I don't have one."

"What? Then show me your wallet. Something with your name on it."

"No way."

"Do as I say . . . I'm here to help you."

She gave me an uneasy look, reached for her bag, hesitating, paused, and reached again. From her wallet she pulled out a credit card and showed me. *Anything you want.* How did a woman with a job like this pass a credit check? Or was it from her past? I checked the signature on the back.

Mari Yamamoto.

No, this could have easily just been a card belonging to a person with that name.

". . . You're going to tell me the truth. Otherwise, I might have to destroy you."

"What do you mean, the truth?"

"You are Ami Ito, aren't you?"

But she just looked at me, confused.

This made no sense.

9

I heard the clicking of nail clippers.

It was a dry sound, set against the humid air of the cramped hostess bar. A lanky man leaned forward in a chair.

"If you clip your nails at night, you won't be there to see your parents when they die," I told the man, busying my hands with my mother's handkerchief. Tying it in knots.

It was a saying that I'd heard a million times as a kid. Looking back, it was so strange. That I would open up to a man who had just bought me a soda. That I would expect anything from a man who waltzed into the bar wearing dirty work clothes, ready to go digging under his nails with a toothpick.

"Fine, considering my folks are dead already."

The man clipped as he spoke. All he had to do was turn away from me, but he wanted to have the last word. Welcome or not.

"Besides, if I don't clip my nails . . ." the man said,

looking up at me. That's how I can remember his face so clearly. A face that was all too proud. That I had woefully misread. "I'll scratch your mother."

I WOKE UP panting violently.

Ami Ito was naked beside me. Or the woman I had thought was Ami Ito, who was actually someone else.

". . . Huh?" I asked. The situation didn't add up. The woman I had thought was Ami Ito gave me a blank stare. Some kind of porn was playing on the TV screen.

"You fell asleep . . . just like that."

"Asleep?"

"Yeah . . . halfway through a text, saying you were going to make me look at someone's picture."

I was stunned.

"For how long?"

"Five minutes. Oh, and . . . you should wipe your face."

I wiped my face with my hand. I was crying.

Wow. I must have been really tired. Crying like that, nothing to be sad about.

I tried to speak but couldn't get the words out. As if the strands that formed my feelings and my manners tangled up and choked me in the process of becoming words. From the bed, she watched me leaning forward in my chair. On the TV, a woman with brown hair was having sex with multiple men.

"If this was happening five years ago, I'd . . ." She stopped abruptly. I waited for her to go on, but she said nothing.

". . . What happened five years ago?"

"Never mind."

"If you start saying something, you may as well finish."

She gave me a blank stare but eventually she flinched.

"If this had happened back then . . . I think I'd probably feel bad."

The room glowed with garish pink lights. It was humiliating.

"Feel bad for you, I mean . . . I had a weakness, or something like that, for guys like you . . . If I saw a sad-looking man, we usually wound up . . . sleeping together . . . That's what they wanted from me. Sometimes I turned them down, only afterwards, I wished that I had done it. For their sake . . . Awful, huh?"

Unsure of what to say to this, I lit a cigarette.

"But, I mean, now, it's different . . . It's been a while since I've met a man like you . . . but I'm not feeling any-thing . . . I guess I've lost the ability to take pity on others . . . Well, what now?"

She looked at me. Like she was two seconds away from stealing my cigarette.

"You've got me here . . . The stuff you're saying makes no sense, and I have no idea why you're here, but either way . . . I'm not going home until you tell me to . . . It's up to you. Whatever you want."

With that, she lay back on the bed.

"If your ex-girlfriend is named Ami Ito, you could just pretend I'm her."

She stared at the ceiling. For some reason, I got the sense that she was really looking towards the sky. Watching the gods. But her line of sight was thwarted. By that shabby ceiling and the seedy pink light fixture dangling there. On the TV screen, the pack of men grew increasingly aggressive.

"*Anything you want*. That's what he told you, right? It's true, too. *You could even kill me*, if you wanted to. It's that kind of a situation, and I'm that kind of a woman . . . When you're with me, you can let everything go. I can usually tell what you guys have in mind . . . So go ahead. Use me to satisfy your deepest, darkest urges . . . Though I suppose I'm being unfair, huh. Women use men to satisfy their darkest urges too."

". . . How'd you wind up doing this?"

"You had to ask me my least favorite question, didn't you," she said, eyes fixed on the ceiling. "Go down to Ikebukuro or Shinjuku at night and ask the same thing to the women you find standing there. You'll get all kinds of different answers. What kind of response would you like? You want to hear about my trauma?"

I stood up. The idea had been to grab her clothes and

toss them on the bed. But when I got a better look at her, lying there naked, my heart sped up a little. Plastic bags from the drugstore scattered around her. The memory that haunted me. Seeing the woman's bathing suit being torn off underwater. How I almost drowned, but I was rescued by the kind stranger. How the harmony of the world was ruined and replaced by the nail clippers and plastic bags from the convenience store. Someone was coming, but he stopped at the fence. Then the kind man, he said to me—

I was tired. What was I saying? There were no bags from the drugstore. Maybe the body of the man hadn't been soaking wet at all, like I had thought. I looked at her, ashamed of myself for the lust that I was feeling. Let everything go? But how? Should I call up a bunch of guys so we can pass her around? Is that how men are supposed to let everything go? I had no memories of seeing anything like that at my mom's club, but I had a feeling that she'd gladly let her customers do things like that to her.

After my mother died, I evidently had symptoms of amnesia. Not so much suppressing memories, as suffering from an acute psychopathology. Like a new hire who stops showing up at work. He remembers leaving his apartment in the morning, but a few days later, he wakes up at some hotel in the country, far from home. The sort of amnesia that they call a fugue state, brought on by extreme stress. Whole days lost, during which he rides the subway and the bullet train and checks into a hotel but remembers none of it.

That man was me. Only I didn't actually go anywhere. I just forgot most of my life up to that point. And I can't say the amnesia did me any good. The memories I wish I could have suppressed were the ones that stayed. But at the time, the memories were strangely blended with images of the ocean, or of a mountain, or of things that I was sure that I had never done, like I was living in a manga.

My mother saw men in our room on the bar's second floor. Sometimes I peeked. If I had to get amnesia, why couldn't this be one of the memories I lost? Some amnesia. When they found her body, hair soaking wet, naked and dead from an overdose, there were condoms left all over her. Left by the men who had gone home, not knowing she was dead. Unable to wait for her to finish showering before sex, the men had led her from the bathroom and slept with her before she had the chance to dry her hair. But if I'd managed to suppress that memory, it hadn't been by swapping it out with my memory of the beach, or by replacing all of those used condoms with the plastic bags from the convenience store. By a strange twist of fate, on the day my mother died, I was far away at nature camp with my elementary school. All my memories of camp had been wiped out by the amnesia, but from what I gathered, I was just a normal kid, nothing to make me stand out from the other kids in any way.

Incredible, I told myself, shaking off the images. If I tied her up right now and made it look like she had hanged herself, the investigation would be over. A woman that the police had been tracking had escaped but found herself caught in a corner, so she hanged herself in a decrepit love hotel. No camera footage either way. All I had to do was text a suicide note to somebody in her contact list. Case closed, before the first division picked it up. If she wasn't Ami Ito, she had to be the woman in the photograph with Kazunari Yoshikawa. If the suspects aren't alive, not much energy goes into an investigation.

"*No, not inside me.*"

The woman onscreen raised her voice. Japanese porn generally blurs out the genitalia, but this video was uncensored. She was held down, mounted and voraciously defiled by the pack of men.

"*Not inside me. Wait, stop, not inside . . .*"

She delivered her lines monotonously. I watched the screen, in a daze. Why did I feel so out of place?

". . . Listen to her," said the woman I had thought was Ami Ito. "Usually, in scenes like this, they have the woman tell the guys to finish off inside her . . . I've done scenes like this myself, I should know."

The woman on screen was almost choking between breaths.

"But not this one . . . they've got her saying no. Most of the time, you have to act and say the opposite of what you mean. But she obviously doesn't want these guys finishing inside of her, so these lines aren't exactly a performance. There's something to them that reflects her actual emotions . . . which makes it even creepier for her to say it like she's some kind of a robot. It's not like she secretly wants him to do it, obviously. But she doesn't not want him to do it either."

The man inside her groaned and came. He really came inside her. Since the video was uncensored, you could tell. When he pulled out, a little semen dripped from her vagina. After saying no again, she glanced down at her vagina and smiled inexplicably. As if intrigued.

"The way it looks to me, she's having fun with them. Amused at how they're treating her like shit . . . You might say that, she's letting them do anything they want. She doesn't care what happens to her body . . . just like me."

My phone lit up. A text from Ichioka. I'd asked him to snap a picture of the photocopy of the photograph of Kazunari Yoshikawa I had forgotten to bring. The resolution was awful, but you could recognize him in the picture.

". . . Take a look at this. That's Kazunari Yoshikawa . . . and that's you."

She examined the photograph, expressionless as ever.

". . . What is this?"

Her voice quivered, ever so slightly.

"We look alike, I'll give you that, but it's not me."

Once again, I almost lost my mind. On closer

examination, the woman in the photo and the woman there with me were similar, but clearly different people. For one, the woman I was with was much younger.

"Is this woman . . . even real?"

". . . Huh?"

"Her face . . . There's something off."

10

"Turns out this Ami Ito is already dead."

Another of our regular morning briefings. We started with this news from Ichioka, but Tozuka had already given me the scoop.

"She was on the lease with Kazunari Yoshikawa and appeared beside him in the photograph, but come to find she bears a striking resemblance to an unidentified body that turned up half a year ago . . . I think we can safely say it's her. We're still waiting on the details, but we know they found her hanging from a rope . . . Needless to say, Ami Ito can't be the one that murdered Kazunari Yoshikawa."

What now? Taking deep breaths in an effort to unclench my heart, I thought things over. This meant that the woman I mistook for Ami Ito was a lookalike, a different person, like she said. But that didn't explain why Kazunari Yoshikawa had written her employer in his planner under "Ami Ito," or why they happened to have such similar faces.

". . . This means we're back to square one," said the police chief, stepping in. "Starting tomorrow, there's gonna be a new task force setting up at Ninagawa Station . . . This case is getting pulled out of our jurisdiction. What happens next is up to headquarters, the first division."

I felt a dull pain in my chest.

"File your findings . . . That'll be all."

We stood up, heavy on our feet. All my energy had left me. I couldn't move. As if all of the blood had emptied from my temples and my head, bringing about a sudden plunge in body temperature.

"Crock of shit," Tozuka said, beside me. "This is your first time with the first division, right? Those guys look down on all the lower jurisdictions . . . Basically everything we've done means nothing now. They'll want to do it all again themselves."

My relationship with Maiko. My trick with Maiko's fingerprints. Once a detective from the first division had a look at things, and questioned Maiko, and took her prints again, my improprieties would come to light.

AGAINST THE LANDSCAPE of the windows of the train, the power lines made a continuous black streak. As if the wires were encircling the train, coiling around the cars.

"I'm not going home until you tell me to . . . It's up to you. Whatever you want."

I could've sworn that the woman I'd thought was Ami Ito said those words, but after I fell asleep again, she vanished from the room. No matter how sleep deprived I was, it wasn't normal to keep nodding off like that. Maybe I'd been drugged. But what would make her do a thing like that?

Pulling myself together, I caught a taxi and opened up Yoshikawa's planner. I saw an address that I hadn't seen before. There was no way that I had simply overlooked it, either. Had "Ami Ito" left it for me? If so, why? The script was obviously different from the sloppy writing on the other pages.

Tomorrow was the end for me. I decided that I may as well check out the address, not expecting it to get me anywhere. My sole remaining options were to help Maiko escape, or to leave everything behind and escape with her.

"Let's just keep going."

My mother told me once. One evening in elementary school, riding with me on the train. Another night when the black power lines strung endless webs outside the windows. Or was I misremembering things?

". . . We're supposed to get off at the next stop . . . but we could keep on riding and go somewhere else, far away from here."

I remember how she sounded then, her voice a little hollow.

"If we don't get off at the next stop, there'll be another. You know that."

Wiping some mud off of my legs, bare from the hem of my shorts to my socks, with the handkerchief my mother gave me that I carried everywhere, I looked up at her beautifully ragged face.

"Shibata, Nawa, Shurakuen . . . other cities, other lives, with Mondays, and Tuesdays . . . and the same kinds of bars, except instead of being called Miyuki, it's Akemi, and the guy you know as Suzuki is named Tanaka . . . No matter how far away you go, it's all the same."

My mother's lips, done up in thick lipstick, trembled faintly.

I could just barely see the track marks on her arms. She should have worn long sleeves.

"I'm afraid your mother's lost control of herself."

With those words, she turned towards me, disheveled hair and all, lips twitching for a moment, before turning back towards the window. In retrospect, I have to wonder if the question she had left unasked was: "Would you like to go alone? I'm getting off at the next stop, but how about you? You could go someplace far away."

The week before, I had seen my father. It was a chance to step out of my life. A chance to break away from this piece of crap red train that I was always riding with my mother.

Now and then, my father met me after school in a

clean suit. He took me to a cafe and told me I could have anything I wanted, but I always picked the cheapest item on the menu, ramune soda. What I really wanted was a meron soda, or banana soda, with a plate of pancakes or naporitan spaghetti. But it felt like a betrayal of my mother.

That day a week before, however, we didn't go to a cafe, but to an unfamiliar house. A house that he had built with his new family.

When I stepped out of my grubby shoes by the door, my dad's new wife greeted me with a smile and a pair of brand-new slippers. I had never worn a pair of slippers in a house before.

The living room had a low table for four and a watery blue area rug accented with pink cushions. Beyond that, there was a giant TV hanging on the wall, so shallow it looked fake. Compared with our messy house, the tatami room above my mother's hostess bar, this room was almost too clean.

"How about living here with us?"

That's what my dad asked me. Maybe he thought that if I saw the place, I'd drop the silent act I used at the cafe and nod approvingly. His facial expression was so serious. I opened my mouth, ready to decline, but for some reason I couldn't get the words out and stopped breathing. As if my physical reflexes had taken over.

I wonder what my father felt when he saw my reaction.

The doorbell rang. Normally his wife would be the one to answer, but he got up instead, I guess to give us both a break. He must have been uncomfortable.

". . . I'm sure that it's confusing," my dad's wife said, "being asked so suddenly."

She smiled. Speaking quietly, conscious of the distance between us. Behind her, I could see a baby sleeping in a tiny bed.

"I'm so impressed, a boy like you . . . What would your mother do without you? You've been so good to her, loyal and supportive. Of course you can't abandon her . . ."

It took some time for me to comprehend the meaning of these mysterious statements.

"It's commendable, really. Protecting your mother like that . . . Such a fine boy."

She said the same thing over and over. As if saying I should stick to what I knew. My father's wife had brought new life into this world. She was blessed. I'm sure she hadn't been expecting me to take my father up on moving in with them, this late in the game. Then what was it? Had something about the sight of me made her uneasy? Did she see me as a greedy little kid? If she wanted to tell me something, this was her chance, just the two of us. But I guess that's why she just kept rambling on like that. I'm not sure if she realized that her roundabout expressions, while stated with the utmost care, backfired with the force of the most naked insult. The thin layer of skin

cream on her hands was a forcefield, her form of protec-
tion; it caught the overhead light and sent it towards me
in a slightly diluted form.

This was all because I failed to say no when my father
made his offer. I was too late. And so I had to suffer through
this speech from her. I was getting pissed. I should have
said no when I had the chance. I had a feeling that this
shame would follow me around for the remainder of my
life. As if the shape of my existence had been settled in
an instant.

My father came back from the door. He had some mail
that had nothing to do with me. For some reason I couldn't
stop staring at the warm light shining off his wife's hands.
Self-conscious as he was, my dad tried to make sense of
the situation. Wanting me to choose, one or the other.
That's how it seemed to me. None of this wishy-washy
back and forth.

Maybe my dad was suffocating on the happiness he
had achieved. He was so happy he felt guilty, and this
made him fixate on me. On his son, getting scuzzier by the
day, in that scuzzy room above the bar, where his scuzzy
ex-wife worked at night. By taking me in, my dad was
trying to hold himself to a higher standard of morality, and
roping in his mediocre wife while he was at it.

Next thing I knew, my mouth had crept into a grin.
This place was way too clean for me. A place this clean
was too precarious. At home, above the bar, it made no

difference whether you spilled soy sauce on the floors. You couldn't hurt them.

What was up with that shallow TV? Ours was the old-fashioned, boxy kind with a glass screen. We used the top of it like a shelf, where we kept stacks of junk mail and an empty piggy bank. You couldn't put a single thing on top of this TV. Ours, meanwhile, didn't even have a remote. We had to change the channels with the dial, but the knob had fallen off, so we had to turn it with a pair of pliers. If it wasn't working, all you had to do was whack it. Could you fix this TV with a firm slap? I had no interest in their sparkly new gadgets. They couldn't take a hit.

Happiness is one thing, but trying to wipe your conscience clean, that's going too far. Why couldn't my dad and his new wife be happy living their clean lives, in their clean neighborhood, with their clean schedules and routines? I had nothing to say, just stood there in the living room. My dad said he would drive me home. I have a hard time remembering my dad's face, but what I do recall is the way his eyes looked at the cafe when he glared at the people who were smoking, even though their smoke wasn't coming towards us. I could feel something in those eyes, something horrifying that was ready to stab into me. He had tossed us aside, his wife and son, and started a new family. What did he want now? To see himself as some kind of perfect person? Drunk on his idea of what he owed me, as a father, he had entangled his young wife, who owed me nothing whatsoever.

Suffice to say, you'd think that I would sympathize with what my mom was saying, riding with her on the train that time. But instead, I had to say something I had no business saying. Had I lost my mind? High on a sense of superiority over her, because I had been asked to live in that clean house, without her?

"Hey, Mom?"

"Yeah?"

"You act like life's so hard."

". . . Huh?"

"But I know that's how you like it."

The train came to a stop. We were at the unmanned station where we were supposed to get off. Mom hesitated for a second, then got off of the train, like always. But then she stood there, in the middle of the platform, unable to move. The setting sun shone dull and bleary, like a stranger, off the clasps of her red handbag, which contained the medicine she had just picked up at the hospital. My mom was crying. It was only a week later that my frail mother died of a drug overdose. They called it an accident, but if you were to reframe it as a murder, like a detective set on questioning every single detail, the murder weapon was none other than the cruel thing I had told her on the train. I may have been away at nature camp when it actually happened, but the murder weapon worked without me there. I was like a murderer with the perfect alibi.

After my mom died, I didn't move in with my dad, but with my grandmother on my mom's side. When I passed the police force entrance exam, he came by with his wife. He was getting up there, but she still looked young. My dad feebly offered his congratulations. His wife cried the entire time. It probably hurt her to recall the rambling speech that she had given me, though seeing for herself that it hadn't stopped me from becoming a "fine young man," she must have felt some combination of relief and joy. Those tears may have been egotistical and self-absorbed, but as I'm sure you can tell, my dad's wife was not an evil person. Her problem was she lived for peace.

I stepped off of the train and followed the directions on my maps app to the address in the planner. Twiddling my mother's handkerchief, in the pocket of my suit. I had fished it out of the bureau in her closet. The one token of her that I kept. When things went from bad to worse, I escaped into sentimentality. The space between the houses widened by degrees, but after I went by a rusty old gas station, I was on a road with nothing but a forest on both sides. It was a quiet road, so straight it looked unnatural. Google Maps was leading me towards a little pond. The trees surrounded me, but there was not a sign in sight.

"Togashi."

What the hell? Was someone trying to fuck with me?
Terrified, I spun around. My pulse was speeding up.
It was Hayama. Right behind me.

11

"What're you doing out here?" Hayama asked me.

I was unable to gather my thoughts.

". . . How'd you find me?" I asked.

"I followed you."

I felt a dull pain in my heart. As usual, Hayama wore a suit cut from expensive fabric, too nice for what he made as a detective. On him, however, it had a nihilistic flair. No sooner had I noticed he was carrying an oddly wrinkled paper bag than he pulled something out of it and tossed it at my feet.

A pair of shoes. The pair I left in the apartment.

The strength drained from my body.

". . . Huh?"

". . . I asked you what you're doing."

Our eyes met. For what could have been a couple seconds or a couple minutes. What was this about? How did Hayama get my shoes?

"I was just . . . taking a walk."

"Skip it. I've been behind you this whole time. *What the hell are you doing?*"

I took a deep breath. My hands were shaking. I told myself to hold still, but Hayama had already seen them trembling.

". . . What's up with these shoes?" I asked him.

"I know they're yours."

"I have no clue what you're talking about . . . cheapo shoes like these."

"There's bird shit on the heels."

He was right. Where had I picked that up? In the parking lot outside INCONSCIENT? There had been pigeon spikes all over the place.

"Last time you were wearing these, I remember thinking, boy his shoes are filthy. Figured that you must've been pretty distracted, to overlook a mess like this . . . And no. They're not my shoes. Don't even ask. If you'd come anywhere near me wearing these, I would have told you to go get a rag. Another thing. The way you walk. The toes of your left shoe bump up against the heel of your right foot. Look, see what I mean?" He pointed at the shoes. "The right side of the toe box of the left shoe is worn down. Topped off with a smidge of bird shit. These shoes are yours."

My heart was pounding. So, had Hayama been there when I found the dead man, soaking wet, in the apartment? How did he manage that? He glanced down at the shoes that I was wearing now. Worn out in the exact same places as the shoes tossed at my feet.

My phone rang out of nowhere. Hayama told me with his eyes to take it. I checked the screen. It was Maiko.

What was she doing? I could've sworn I'd told her not to call me. If they looked through my call history, my connection to her would be clear.

Trying in vain to steady my breath, I picked it up. Her voice was shaky.

—*A detective named Hayama was just here.*

"Huh?"

—*I tried giving him the alibi we made up together . . . I'm not sure if my old boss did such a good job after all.*

Any remaining strength drained from my body.

". . . Is that all?"

—*He didn't take my fingerprints . . .*

I realized the call was dead. I had to get away from here. It was all that I could think about. But then I looked up at Hayama, there in front of me.

"That apartment where we found Kazunari Yoshikawa."

He paused to take a haul off of his cigarette and exhaled white smoke. I hadn't even seen him light the thing.

"Remember how I told you that the placement of the furniture was strange? . . . Especially the TV. Most people have the TV in a spot where they can watch it while they're eating, or maybe see it from their bed. But they had it set up so that you had to get up from the bed or dinner table and go stand in front of it."

The smoke coming from the cigarette in Hayama's right hand was so straight it looked unnatural.

"It'd be one thing if he never watched TV. But that apartment had a subscription to cable, until three months ago . . . The only explanation is that the interests of the people living there had changed. Unless, that is, *there was a change in the people living there*."

I did my best to follow what Hayama was telling me, trying to pull myself back down to earth.

"In the corner, off the foot of the bed, the best place for a TV in the bedroom, there was nothing on the floor. But the carpeting was dented. Three noticeable divots. Something with three legs had been sitting there awhile. Most electrical appliances have four legs. Three is odd. I realized that it must have been a camera. On a tripod. Judging from the depth of the divots in the carpeting, it must have been a pretty heavy-duty camera, like the pros use. Yoshikawa was a rope artist. Stands to reason he would film himself. We're still questioning people in the BDSM world, but no one wants to work with the police. I doubt any of the testimonies will be useful. But if Yoshikawa filmed this stuff, he might show up in a commercially available video. We're checking with some people in the pornography industry. Not just the big-league outfits, but the folks who do it in groups, as a hobby, too, so it'll take a little time. But there's no doubt in my mind that we'll get something eventually."

I gave Hayama a blank stare.

"Remember how there were a bunch of those conservative magazines on the floor of the apartment?"

Magazines? All I saw were Maiko's favorite things. I didn't remember any magazines.

"Seems like Yoshikawa had some pretty sweaty hands. There are dark marks from the oils of his fingers on the edges of the pages. I tried reading one of his books, holding it the same way. And guess what? I got sick of it in the same spot as him, where the marks left by his fingers stopped."

Hayama puffed his cigarette. At the cuff of his right sleeve, I caught a glimpse of the bracelet of crystal prayer beads on his wrist.

"One of those junky books that blames everything on China and Korea. This led me to believe that Yoshikawa didn't gravitate towards trashy politics or trashy culture, as it were, but something more authentic, or traditional . . . Didn't the owner of the fetish club you visited with Ichioka tell you? Yoshikawa said he liked to let the rope call the shots. He tied his knots to satisfy the rope. I think it's safe to say that Yoshikawa was an odd case, not like most other rope artists. Kinbaku, rope, conservatism . . . What links them all is Shinto."

". . . Shinto?"

"Don't you know? In kinbaku, you're only supposed to use rope made from hemp. As in the cannabis plant, a major source of clothing in the old days in Japan. Hemp rope is inseparable from Japanese culture and religion. The cannabis plant has been cultivated on this soil since the Jomon period, when decorative earthenware was made by winding cord around the outside of clay vessels. The braided shimenawa ropes that you find hanging at a Shinto shrine, also hemp, serve as a boundary between the everyday world and the spirit realm. In Shinto, hemp rope is used to mark off sacred spaces. We find this in sumo wrestling, which is in fact a Shinto ritual, where only the highest-ranking wrestlers, the yokozuna, are allowed to wear the ceremonial belt made from white cord. The wrestlers toss salt in the ring and stomp their feet to ward off evil spirits. And guess what? The Association of Shinto Shrines does grassroots work for conservative causes and drums up votes for conservative politicians."

Hayama blinked a few times, but his face betrayed no emotion.

"I visited several of the shrines in the vicinity of the apartment where the body was discovered. Sure enough, people there had seen Yoshikawa on the grounds, closely observing the shimenawa at the shrine, or the ways the ropes were tied around the sacred trees. He also had conversations with an old man who visits the shrine daily. Mostly small talk, nothing special, though he talked enough it'd fill reams and reams of paper if we put it in the record. Out of everything I heard, two things caught my attention. Firstly, he told the man, 'It gives me this oppressive feeling, just short of clinical anxiety, every time I leave the house, which is a real nuisance. It's a struggle getting out the door.' The second thing was even stranger. 'You should see the view outside my house. Too bad I'm not a Christian.' Strange things to say. Yoshikawa's apartment faces a park. Nothing oppressive to be found. It'd be another thing if he had some negative experience with parks, but once he's 'out the door,' there's nothing but the park to see in both directions. But what if the apartment where we found the body wasn't his? Think about it. Calling it a 'real nuisance' makes it sound like someone else's fault. And 'oppressive' brings to mind either a tall new building just outside, or the construction of something big . . . I looked into it. But at the time when Yoshikawa and the old man had these conversations, there were over thirty apartment buildings in the area. It'd be a major undertaking to investigate them all in person. Perusing photos on the internet, however, I found one spot that stood out from the rest. I checked it out. And what did I find but a little rundown building with a brand-new high-rise right outside. And on the other side, through the windows at the back, you could see three telephone poles, just like in the photo. Telephone poles come in all different shapes and sizes, but some of them look like crosses, right? These poles were of the cross-shaped variety. The cross, of course, is at the very top, so pretty small, but they look almost like three misshapen crosses, set up for three criminals. According to the Bible, three people were crucified, Jesus and two others. The sun goes down behind his building in such a way that the poles, lit from behind, send cross-shaped shadows through the windows. 'Too bad I'm not a Christian.' Three crosses, symbols of the West, outside the window of a man obsessed with traditional Japanese ropework. I asked myself, could this be it? I showed some locals Yoshikawa's picture. They confirmed that he had lived there. The door to his apartment was unlocked. The place was empty, but it had that smell, you know the one I mean. The strange reek of a dead body. *The body must have only just been taken away.* There was a piece of paper on a messy desk. 'I did it. I accept my fate entirely and give my life.' . . . That's what it said. Though isn't that a little strange? A suicide note, but no body . . . This gave me an idea. *What if there were multiple culprits?* One who tried to pin the crime on the dead body, and another one who prevented them from doing so. *In other words, each of the culprits thought a different person was the criminal* . . . A case like that would be unprecedented . . . But then I stumbled on this pair of shoes. I was surprised . . . knowing that they must belong to you."

I was dumbstruck, staring at Hayama. This whole time, beyond my reach, the case had been developing, in his hands, out of mine. If you thought of it as some kind of a story, *it was like I had been cut almost entirely from the plot.*

And meanwhile, behind my back—

"Let's talk about Maiko Kirita."

It hurt to breathe, as if something had pierced my chest.

"One of the cards in Yoshikawa's planner was from Maiko Kirita. We know that Kazunari Yoshikawa was an alias. But I noticed something strange about her name. Break apart the characters for Maiko, and you get 'girl wearing hemp.' For a case like this, that's a *pretty big coincidence.* Wouldn't you say? I figured that it has to be another alias."

It became difficult for me to continue standing.

"I paid Maiko a visit. Seems like the alibi she handed you was bogus. But because she's working as an escort, she didn't want to tell the truth . . . so I pressed her on it. Turns out she had another alibi, *but it was a bit too perfect* . . . Something else you'd like to tell me?"

It took me everything I had just to look back at Hayama.

"Let me refresh your memory. In our search of the apartment where we found Yoshikawa, we came across a framed picture of him and Ami Ito. But none of the clothes we found there matched her taste. Another woman must have lived there. Here's the thing, though. If Yoshikawa had been going back and forth between the apartment where we found his body and the place I found the note, we can deduce that he was sharing the apartment where we found the photograph of him and Ami Ito with another woman. Think about it. What kind of woman would let that slide? It would take a special kind of pervert to go in for that. Out of all the different possibilities, the most likely one is that Ami Ito has been dead for a while now, and that Yoshikawa and the other woman were living in that place together, haunted by the crime. That would explain the solemn air of that apartment. You'll recall that Ichioka did a survey of unidentified bodies, focusing on ones that looked like they had hanged to death. Well, I'm the one who told him to. And by the way, I noticed something you might like to hear about the fashion tastes of the woman who was living in that place with Yoshikawa."

Hayama looked straight at me.

"She has the same style as Maiko Kirita."

I was standing there with a blank look on my face, staring back at Hayama, but something compelled me to move around and laugh. And loudly, too. Not like there was anything to laugh about. I made a fist around my mother's handkerchief, in my pocket.

"Hayama," I said. No idea what I was going to say next. "You're just as tough as everybody says. Can't say I feel too hot running into you out here! But, but yeah, I've got something that you're gonna have a hard time beating."

I was practically screaming. Had I gone crazy? I felt myself breaking away.

"The darkness! The darkness of uncertainty! Hahaha! Get ready, because you're about to see what a little bit of darkness humming with uncertainty can do."

Run away, I told myself. I had to run away with Maiko, as far as I could go. Away from this man. From this world. Away from my life. Let Hayama track me down, with his fancy deductive reasoning. Let him pick apart the story of my life. Let him chase me to my dying day.

"Togashi," said Hayama.

The wind blew, making the trees around us sway.

"*This is not the sort of case you think it is.* If the videos that Yoshikawa made turn up, it's going to mean a world of trouble. All kinds of things that have been hidden from the surface of the earth will come to light. *This is another kind of case entirely.* Go on, tell me everything you know. If we could only put our heads together."

"What are you saying?"

"Togashi," Hayama said again. I detected kindness in his voice. For a second, I felt like I could cry. The trees around us swayed. The wind was picking up.

"I'll wait a day. Okay? Before you turn yourself in, talk to me."

12

I stared blankly through the doorway at Maiko.

How did I make it to her place? The only thing I could remember was the fact I took a taxi. As I stepped out of my shoes, I realized I was holding the other pair of shoes and left them by the door. Both pairs. As if two of me were stepping into her apartment. Maiko's sneakers sat beside them.

". . . Did you hear from Detective, uh . . . Hayama?"

"Yeah."

Maiko stared at me. With that gorgeous face of hers. Purple sweats, top to bottom.

". . . So he didn't take your prints?"

"Not yet. But even if he had . . . it wouldn't matter."

". . . Why?"

"Because I don't have fingerprints anymore."

I looked at Maiko, confused. Her hair was wet.

". . . What?"

"They're gone . . . way back, I had them surgically

removed. Palm prints too. So there's no way that my prints could show up anyhow."

My pulse was speeding up.

"How come you didn't speak up when I told you I was swapping out the prints?"

"I mean . . ." Maiko looked bewildered. "I knew you wanted to do something nice for me . . . so I didn't want to stop you."

All I could do was give her another long, blank stare. What was she saying? What the hell was she telling me?

"Hold on, do you realize how much of a risk I had to take to get those other prints? Any idea?"

"I was bad . . . Are you going to punish me?"

". . . Huh?"

"Unless I'm punished . . . I won't learn my lesson."

She looked at me with a twinkle in her eye. What was she saying? This was not a time for sexy roleplaying, but nevertheless, Maiko came closer, eyes half-closed, and brought her lips to mine, sticking her tongue out just a little. She kissed me. Her tongue stroked the inside of my mouth. As if consoling me for what had happened. Though what had happened was her fault.

". . . Look."

She picked up my right hand and placed it between her legs. She was incredibly wet. So wet that it was soaking through her purple underwear and dripping down the inside of her thigh. It split into a second streak and vanished in the hollow of her knee.

"I've been waiting, saving it all, for you . . . I haven't touched myself since the last time you were here."

I wrapped my arms around her and laid her on the bed. What was I doing? This was neither the time nor the place. I knew that I'd regret it all the second that I came.

"Hold on a sec."

From a shelf beside the bed, Maiko pulled down a length of rope. Her wet hair fell across the bed. She looped the rope around her waist.

". . . Peel off my underwear. Tie me up like the bad girl that I am."

I took off Maiko's underwear, practically tearing it away. Her white skin was already damp with sweat, so beautiful I had to catch my breath. Recalling the rope artist at the fetish club, I crossed her hands behind her back and bound them tightly together.

"Just . . . yeah, that's it. Mhm, yeah."

I passed the rope under her breasts so that it lifted them up gently.

"You're supposed to go above them first, so that's backwards, but you can just, uh . . ."

I passed the rope above her breasts and tied a knot behind her back. It pinched into her breasts from above and below.

Now that she couldn't move her arms, I dragged my

tongue across her nipples. Maiko screamed. She was unable to escape. Tied down.

"Mhm . . . ahh."

I put a finger into her vagina. She had already soaked the sheets beneath her.

"Ah, ahhh! No, ugh, I'm gonna come . . . don't watch me, oh, I'm close . . . ah, ahh!"

Maiko was screaming.

"Don't watch me! No, ah, ah, don't look!"

Both arms restrained, Maiko closed herself around my finger and arched her back. She started shivering and spasmed like she had been zapped. Sinking deep into the mattress, she looked into my eyes. As if to tell me, through the twinkle in her eye, how quickly I had made her come, tied up like this; to show me that she knew I had been watching the whole time. Her wet hair was an ocean. She was mine.

"This rope, see, it's made from hemp . . . cannabis."

Maiko told this to me in a breathy voice, as I fondled her soft breasts and licked her neck.

"If wild animals eat cannabis, mhmm, they get silly and run off . . . Why do you think, uh, yeah, a plant like that exists?"

". . . Not sure."

"It could easily be poisonous, but do you, oh, mhm, do you know why cannabis isn't strong enough to poison you? Because . . . mhm, yeah, it's too nice."

I put another finger into Maiko, who could barely move, and kissed her hair.

"Ah! Mhm, yeah, it's nice, nice to the animals, mhmm, ah, ah, just a little, just a bite for them . . . a little bite is fine, but it's bad for them to eat it all. Ahhh! You, though . . ."

Maiko kissed me. Passionately.

"Today, I want you to devour me . . . you can even put it in my ass . . . you can totally go crazy."

Panting heavily, I tied up Maiko's feet.

"Don't bother," she said.

With those twinkling eyes, Maiko looked at me, a little bashful, but sort of smiling too, then opened her legs wide. Slender legs. It was all that I could do to breathe.

"Once you're inside of me, I'll wrap my legs around you, huh, and squeeze you hard, like you're tied up."

I put myself inside of her. As soon as I was in, Maiko locked her legs around my waist. She had me now. I felt myself go up into the clouds.

"No, ah, not again . . . Don't look at me."

"Maiko, Maiko."

"I'm gonna come . . . *Ahhhhhh!*"

I kept on going, in a trance. Over and over, Maiko closed herself around my penis, soaking me and the bed with her wetness.

"Maiko."

"Oh . . . oh."

"Why won't you look at me?"

"Ah, ahh!"

"Don't look away."

Still going at it, I turned Maiko's face toward mine.

Just as I thought.

Now she looked straight at me, breathing hard. Tears running down her face.

". . . You're crying."

I kept on going, even harder. Maiko was crying, panting heavily.

"How could I have missed a thing like that . . . I guess this means you don't want anything to do with me."

"Ah, ahhhhh."

"So, what . . . I've been assaulting you . . . this whole time?"

Gasping for air, Maiko gave me the saddest look.

"But know what? I don't think you're crying because you hate it . . . those tears—"

—I feel for you, truly.

I felt the dull prod of a pistol being pressed into the back of my head.

The air conditioner was making an exhausted, clanking sound. I stopped thrusting myself in and out of Maiko. Most guys, under the circumstances, would have been thrown into a state of shock, but what puzzled me the most was how relaxed I was.

"All right," I told the man behind me. ". . . I get it now . . . at least half of it."

Maiko was really crying.

I was seriously confused about why I wasn't nervous. The gun was firm against my skull.

". . . If I had killed the woman who looked just like Ami Ito, would you have let me go?"

—*That's right.*

I thought about the woman I had been with at the love hotel. The way she had been staring at the shabby ceiling, watching the gods. I didn't want to kill her. If it came to that, I'd sooner kill myself than have her die.

"Wait." I took a deep breath. Not risking a look. "How can you pull the trigger without a finger?"

—*Look again. It's the middle one I'm missing.*

"Keep going," Maiko said. She was still crying. "At least you'll feel good, when you go."

I was amazed to find myself fucking her again. Amazed at my total lack of fear. I felt myself break free, my pleasure coming to a peak. At this point, I stopped caring about the rest of the world.

". . . Great," I said to myself, savoring the irony. "I've always wanted to do something to redeem my mother. And now . . ."

—*Shall I wait for you to finish?*

I smiled wryly.

"Hah . . . wait."

The gun pulled away from my head and struck my temple as a wave of heat crashed over me. Was it a whirlpool? The bedsheets swung into a spiral. As I neared the edge and slipped into its center, my neck snapped in a strange direction. My face was drenched with blood, but I somehow felt no pain. My essence, or my spirit . . . was still present. Thinking didn't help. My vision narrowed to a point. Before the horror of death takes over, I need to, quickly, find some—body?

Interlude

AN OLDER MAN lay on his back, hooked up to tubes. Bedridden in the hospital, at the end of his life.

Unable to focus his vision on the bleary smear of lights that spread across the ceiling, he thought about his younger days. About the girl who had come into his psychiatric practice years ago, when he was in his fifties. She had been struggling with self-harm.

". . . How about taking this doll home with you?"

What had made him offer it to her?

He had to wonder. He was a family man, but for the first time in years, he was dizzied by intense sexual desire.

Once, walking through town, he had seen a woman in revealing clothes and watched her with a gaze that went beyond momentary lust. His gaze contained a hint of violence. As the woman stepped into a sex club, he got a little tense. Just go inside, he thought, unaware of how the sex industry operates. If he just gave her lots of money, he could grab her hair, whether she liked it or not, and come at her from behind—but he was much too serious a man for that and laughed it off, leaving the club behind him. It was just an impulse that had slipped past his defenses. He was sure he would forget it ever happened.

The doctor handed her the floppy doll, a doll of a young girl. Just a thing that had been laying around the office. But somehow the doll reminded him of the woman in revealing clothes that he had seen that time in town.

"This happens," he told her gently, glancing at the bruises on her arms. "It's what happens when you point the rage inside you, at yourself . . . So next time you want to harm yourself . . . just use this doll."

She was a pretty girl. He was no pedophile, nothing of the sort, but gazing at her bruised arms for what felt like an eternity, he felt butterflies in his stomach. Girls like her showed up from time to time. Dangerous girls, who made him worry for their future. She was only eleven years old, but already so beautiful her young body exuded a promise of sensuality.

She returned to his office two weeks later. He asked how things were going with the doll. She looked refreshed; the bruises on her arms were gone.

". . . Here."

The sight of the doll wiped the smile off his face. It was stuffed with needles. So many there was no place left to stab.

"Look at her," she said. "Poor thing."

The doctor made sure not to betray his arousal through his gestures or his tone. The young lady beheld the doll as if it were a victim, though she had been the one who pushed the needles in. The doctor realized that he had made a terrible mistake. The treatment had been his bright idea, but it was going in the wrong direction.

He decided, however baselessly, that this was all for the best. If it meant stopping a pretty girl like her from doing damage to herself, why not let something else take the blow. Even if that something was the world in its entirety.

And now, as he lay dying, he remembered watching the girl leave his office. Looking back, his life had been a life without exceptional strain. In the grand scheme of things, he had been fortunate indeed, never deviating once from the moral sensibilities around which his life was organized. Now, in the final hour, it was getting hard to breathe, and though he pressed the call button repeatedly, his hand suddenly stopped. Who was that? Was it her? He could have sworn the girl, his patient from so many years ago, was there, before his eyes, on her way out of the room. What was the meaning of this? The girl passed through the threshold, but before she vanished in the darkness of another room, she turned around. Looking back at him with a blank expression.

"Coming?" she asked, but the old doctor had already lost consciousness.

"Come on, let's play."

The light changed, and the man pressed on the gas. Where was he driving, in the middle of the night?

These roads were unfamiliar. It's possible that he might get his bearings if the light were better, but there were no lights out here on the backroads.

Once, long ago, a fortune teller told him that he had a slight ability to connect with the spirit world. He had never seen a ghost or felt a strange sensation passing down a road or through a building that supposedly was haunted, but the unexpected reemergence of the thought left him disturbed. Lately, it had been on his mind almost every day. But the way it had popped up just now, almost like it had been waiting, gave him an eerie feeling. The girl had never been inside his car before.

He worked by day at a high school, as a substitue history teacher, but at night he drove out to a BDSM club the next town over. For a set fee, he could have his way with a submissive woman, within limits. It was rarely enough for him, but he told himself that it was fine. Best to leave his deviant inclinations to the realm of fantasy. One day, however, the owner of the club introduced him to a girl. She was only seventeen, and absolutely gorgeous.

"I had a feeling you'd like her. Go ahead, just for a minute. I know you'll be gentle."

If you're thinking that he used this girl to act out fantasies about sassy schoolgirls looking for attention in their leggy uniforms, you're wrong. He taught at a boys' school, after all. He paid for her, spending no small sum of money. After that, he saw her regularly. When they were done, he always tried to give her money for a ride home, but she insisted on walking.

He tied her up with ropes of hemp and flicked her with a whip. She shivered and squirmed. Like she was begging him to let her go, but also goading him along. He ravished her repeatedly.

Pretty soon, he fell into a more basic routine, where he tied only her hands and then had sex with her. This became his preference over more involved S&M. He devoured her pale body. It was all that mattered. To continue meeting up with her at hotels, he took on huge amounts of debt. On most days, he gorged himself on family life at home, but one night a week, he gorged himself on the pleasures of his other life with her. With a bit more money, he told himself, he could have been happy. His wife's parents paid for a new house. They had a party on the pristine balcony, everyone cheering with delight, but that night, his wife received a photograph. A snapshot of him ravaging the girl like a madman. Her face had been blacked out. It was obviously amateur. Taken with a timer.

His family fell apart. The photo had been sent to the school too. He lost his job. It was either the vice principal or someone from the board of education who had told him he was lucky that he hadn't been arrested. Yet as harshly as these men rebuked him, he could see a trace of envy in their eyes.

The man asked her to meet him at a hotel. She was smiling.

". . . Forgive me," she said.

"Huh?"

"Time for a spanking?"

What was she saying? Because of what she'd done, he had lost everything. A spanking? Did she think that that would solve things? Make it all better?

The man restrained her. For the first time in a while, he tied up more than just her wrists, using the position that she found the most humiliating, the shrimp tie. He bound her arms behind her back and passed the rope again under her beautiful breasts, lifting them up, then lay her on her back and crossed and bound her ankles, tightening the ropes so that her feet were pulled towards her face and exposed her vagina.

"Ah, ah, ahh, ahhhhh!"

That night, the man used all of his S&M toys on the girl, giving her everything he had. He came multiple times. The final time, he was sure that he had killed her.

The sort of S&M he knew was meant to "break" a woman. The goal was for the more deviant aspects of a woman's sexuality, things she normally kept hidden, to be revealed *with her help*. But that night, he was the one being unleashed. There was no telling how far his violent sexual tendencies would go. He almost had to look away.

And yet the girl still wanted more. He could have sworn that he had actually killed her. But from a place of puzzling kindness, she consoled the tired man with clumsy words of reassurance. He was the one on the brink of exhaustion. In a daze, he stared at her.

After that, the two of them lost touch. He assumed that she had other men. That last time, he couldn't for the life of him recall how she had gotten up and left the room.

The man worked at a cram school for a while, but word got out about his past and he was asked to leave. He got by doing temp work, running deliveries or attracting customers for bars, before eventually landing a full-time job at a pachinko parlor. He failed to reconcile with his wife, but once a year he had a chance to see his son. He paid for sex plenty of times after that, but he never lost control again, the way he had with her. He was a shell of the man he used to be. Some vital energy had been lost through his experience with the girl. A piece of him was gone, surrendered permanently.

Still, the man said to himself. *My life may be in*

shambles, but I don't regret any of what happened. On my deathbed, I'll be thinking about that final night with her.

He came to a main road. Finally, he thought. But as he turned, he saw the headlights of a speeding truck.

Part II

1

"Sounds like the case is closed," said the police chief.

Expressionless. His office was nonsmoking, but he smoked anyway. A slight twist to his lips.

"So the rope artist, Kazunari Yoshikawa . . . was killed by one of our detectives, Mikiya Togashi. He must have seen Yoshikawa as some kind of threat. After Togashi killed him, he killed himself, using a non-police firearm he picked up somewhere. His choice of venue for the suicide was a pond on the outskirts of town. Shot himself in the temple and fell right into the water. That's how the first division sees it . . . Sound believable?"

"Not to me," I said.

The chief gestured with his hands, telling me to smoke.

"Alright, Hayama, tell me what you think."

My cigarette pulled a new curtain of smoke around the room. Misty and white. Life goes on after the death of an acquaintance. Days which Togashi had never known. Entire scenes.

"Togashi was a detective . . . so if he was going to kill Yoshikawa, he'd take pains to make it look like a robbery. Yoshikawa was an alias, after all. Togashi would know that he could kill a man like that and get away with it. They could file a missing persons report, sure, but as long as there wasn't a body, the police would have nothing to go by. He'd never leave the body there."

"But you noticed something, right? That he was acting strange."

"At first it was so subtle, it only clicked after the fact . . . He left the crime scene for a smoke, holding a pack of cigarettes. It'd be one thing if he did this all the time, but every time I saw him smoking after that, he didn't pull out the pack until he'd left the building . . . Going outside for a smoke, you're basically playing hooky, so you need to play it cool. Nobody waves the pack around for all to see. So why'd he pull the pack out of his pocket that one time? It's the sort of unnatural move that he might make unconsciously, trying to hide that he had just slipped his hand, or something else, into his pocket. But two days had passed already since Yoshikawa died, so he would've had plenty of time already to dispose of the incriminating evidence. He must have noticed something out of place and acted, in a fit of panic, to protect the perpetrator. That's how I see it anyway."

Hayama was done. The chief looked satisfied.

"Togashi's shoes were in that other apartment you

discovered. You say it smelled like death. There was that unsigned suicide note as well. But when you had a look around, the place was empty, like after somebody moves out. And who was on the lease? Kazunari Yoshikawa. Signed with the alias. Which means the man was juggling two places. What do you make of that?"

"I'm not sure. Togashi left his shoes behind because he escaped through the window. Somebody must have walked in while he was there. Yoshikawa was long gone. Somebody else showed up to see him."

The chief had Togashi's suicide note on his desk. A sheet of printer paper in a plastic baggie. Typed on a computer:

I'm responsible for everything. Kazunari Yoshikawa came after me, so I killed him. Though why he was after me, I'm unable to say. I have a dark past I've been hiding from you all. A darkness I was unable to control. I hope that it will vanish with my death.

It had come to light that as a child, Togashi had been hospitalized for amnesia. Beside his body they had found the bronze sculpture of a bird, glazed with white enamel. The blood had been wiped off, but a luminol test revealed traces of hemoglobin. Without a doubt this was the weapon used to murder Yoshikawa. It had Togashi's prints on it. Though all that meant was that his fingers had been on it at some point in time.

The baggie with the suicide note fluttered in the white tobacco smoke. Perhaps the link between the crime at hand and bondage made this sheet of paper look, at least to me, like it was suffocating. My eyes were itchy, which I blamed on my new contacts. I blinked several times and looked up again, to find the chief was staring back at me.

". . . Unfortunately, the guys in the first division won't listen to a word we say. They want to sweep this case under the rug, forget the fact the culprit was a cop. They have bigger things to worry about. That slasher case, you know, the 'Man in the Coat,' is taking up all of their resources. A couple of days ago, the guys we had been working with got transferred over there . . . but that's not all. I think what really did it for them was the photograph of the dead body that we think was Ami Ito."

The chief lowered his voice.

"They're all too glad to leave this case behind them. *As if they think it's better left unsolved* . . . You used to be with the first division, Hayama. You must have some kind of beef with them. I'm getting ready to retire myself, with no plans to launch a new career in the private sector. I've been divorced twice, no kids, no young detective in the family to take over my legacy. Once I'm out, I'm moving down to Nagasaki with my sweetheart, the bartender at this place where I'm a regular. She and I are going to take it easy for a change . . . Anyway."

Listening to him talk, I couldn't help but smile. We hadn't spoken much before, but it turned out that the chief was an odd duck. I had no grudge against the first division myself, but I wasn't rushing to conclusions, either.

"Hayama, I want you to take care of this. I'll assume complete responsibility."

"Okay," I said. I nodded, steadying my breath. "I know I saw Togashi scoping out the place where he supposedly killed himself, but if you factor in that body vanishing from the apartment, I think we can assume that someone was behind the scenes, pulling the strings. Otherwise it doesn't add up."

". . . In what sense?"

"At first, it seemed to me like there were several different people trying to frame each other. But I don't see it that way anymore. This was the product of a single mind . . . the restless nihilism of somebody who's lost contact with reality, or who views reality as a mere inconvenience . . . That's the impression that I get."

". . . Why's that?" asked the chief.

"Because I'm the same way."

The chief was mildly amused by this. For an instant, his gaze fell on the translucent prayer beads on my wrist.

"I think I know the way you feel. Are you surprised to be getting orders like this from a guy like me? You must have heard the talk. I'm an honest worker, serious to a fault . . . That's the way the guys on the force talk about me, right? Well, it's true. But a few years back, I sort of changed."

"What happened?"

I couldn't help but ask him. Though I wasn't really curious.

The chief snubbed out his cigarette. A little melancholy.

"I got sick of it. Doing the same old thing."

2

Maiko Kirita opened the door, looking at me like she was afraid.

"You probably thought the case was closed, but actually it's nowhere close to over. We're going to need your fingerprints."

The door to her apartment shut behind me. Kirita just stood there, looking at me. Wearing purple sweats and a beige cardigan. The only shoes left by the door were an unlikely pair of sneakers.

"The search isn't concerned with you, not yet. But I'm convinced . . . they'll find your prints all over that apartment. DNA, too."

I pulled out a sheet of paper. The special kind we use to collect fingerprints and handprints.

"Just give me your hands."

I grabbed her wrists. Ready to use force if necessary. The moment Kirita resisted, I pressed her against the wall. She had this aggrieved, sorrowful look on her face. It was beautiful.

". . . Though you know, I could cover for you, that's an option too."

Kirita stared at me. Tears streamed down her face. She had just showered. Her hair was wet.

". . . I don't have any fingerprints. Handprints either."

"I knew it. Do you remember the last time that we spoke, how I forgot my bag and had you grab it? Well, I checked it for prints, but there was nothing. Togashi filed someone else's prints instead of yours . . . What would possess him to do that?"

". . . I'll tell you everything."

Kirita led me into the apartment. A rich, sweet smell wafted from her hair. The table was clear. Without asking for permission, I lit a cigarette. The place already smelled like tobacco. She didn't smoke. Who did?

". . . I think I've mentioned that I used to work in the sex industry?"

"Yeah."

"One time, I got paired up with Kazunari Yoshikawa, the man that you found dead. He said he had another job for me . . . that he would pay me all this money to sleep with some other guy, but I had to film it, too."

Kirita's eyes twitched. She was frightened.

"I turned him down, but he pressured me. Just once, he said. Film the two of you, just once, and I won't bug you anymore. The other guy looked pretty tame. It felt like I didn't have a choice. So I slept with him, and filmed it . . . though I had no idea that he was Detective Togashi."

Her voice was trembling. I was surprised. She didn't look like she was lying.

"I guess Yoshikawa used the video to blackmail Togashi. Maybe he wanted confidential information. I have no idea. One day, Togashi showed up saying he would hide me from the police. That the investigators found my name card in the room with Yoshikawa's body. He said I was in trouble, so he'd taken it upon himself to submit someone else's fingerprints as mine . . . even though I have no prints to take. I didn't want to be involved or think about it anymore, so I said nothing."

"What happened to your fingerprints?"

"I wanted to kill myself, but I couldn't go through with it. I was feeling pretty empty, though. I heard somewhere that you could get your prints surgically removed, so I tried it, for the heck of it. Almost like getting a tattoo. I wanted to vanish from existence. That's where I was at . . . Anyway, here's the video of me and Togashi."

Kirita pulled out a flash drive and plugged it into a brand-new laptop. When the connector was inserted, the computer made a trembling sound.

It started in the middle. Togashi was on top of Kirita,

smothering her. No sound. Kirita flailed her arms and occasionally glanced to the side, towards the camera. It was hidden. The video was short, ending abruptly.

So Togashi had been with her. I somehow felt relieved. Nothing could be worse than dying at the hands of a woman you had never been with. But if he'd been with her, in a sense he had it coming. How's that for reasoning?

". . . Nice try. That video proves without a doubt that you've been lying."

". . . Huh?"

"Get a load of those socks. They're filthy. I know he came here once without his shoes on. You know it, I know it. But on the day that he showed up without shoes . . ."

I looked Kirita right in the eye.

"Yoshikawa was already dead."

Kirita didn't even flinch. She faked a smile.

". . . That isn't proof of anything. His socks could have just been dirty. You can't pinpoint what day it was."

"That's true."

"Who do you think you are, anyway, coming in and trying to disprove every word I say?"

I was flustered. Kirita was staring at me. With those big, beautiful eyes. I had to take a different tack. So I sighed like I was out of patience.

". . . You can spare me the excuses. All you had to tell me was you didn't know that Togashi filed someone else's fingerprints under your name. You could have told me anything, blamed it all on him. But instead you sit me down to watch this sexy video and tell me a big story. Clearly you're hiding something."

I steadied my breath. This was far more than I liked to talk.

"We know this video was filmed after Yoshikawa died. Togashi has you in his arms, but you're looking at the camera. Which means you filmed it for somebody else to see . . . somebody who said another curious detective might come by. And when he did, it was your job to seduce him. It's all coming together now."

"Are you saying that I lured you here?" asked Kirita, taking the same tone as me. "But that you knew it wouldn't work? No . . . that can't be it. Pretty strange, the way you changed your whole demeanor. First, you put your hands all over me. Then you start acting like an angry husband, saying all this stuff that makes no sense. I guess you thought that getting me to confess and switch teams would be easy. You thought I'd solve the case for you. You're a funny detective, know that? But maybe there's hope for you yet."

"Huh?"

"Want to see it again?"

"See what?"

"The video of me getting screwed by Togashi."

I wonder what kind of a face I made. Kirita forced

another smile. She went over to the bed and pulled a length of rope out of a drawer.

"Kinbaku started in Japan . . . back in the Edo period, the time of the samurai. At first, the police used these knots to tie up criminals . . . and over time, a bunch of different styles appeared, so they could switch it up depending on the crime and social standing of the criminal. Japanese people are weirdly particular about the way things are tied up."

Pretending to be bashful, Kirita took off her cardigan. The softness of her breasts was apparent through her tank top. I could see her purple brassiere through the white cotton. The rope passed through her fingers.

"They used to put the criminals on display, for all to see. People saw it as a form of entertainment. They got excited seeing bodies, men and women alike, tied up with rope. The bodies were exposed, out in the open, so nothing stopped people from looking . . . Rope was used for torture, too, to make people confess."

Kirita passed the rope around her body. She was toying with me.

". . . Ropes started to show up in the kabuki theater. These days women aren't allowed to be kabuki actors, but in the beginning, it was all women onstage. The audience loved any scene where somebody got restrained and tortured. Anyway . . ."

Kirita gave me another of those smiles.

"Maybe you can follow through with your original idea, and use this rope to get me to confess. Torment me, violate me, until I lose control. I'll let you be my master . . . Want to try?"

I looked at Kirita. Rope wound around her body. Smiling at me. What was her deal? She came across as innocent, but there was something else afoot. A strange sensation shivered its way through me. Something more akin to loss than joy.

"Cut it out."

"Why? Too much for you?"

"I'm realizing that the only way to get you to confess is to get personally involved. You're much tougher than I thought . . . but I've given up on getting personally involved with anyone."

I went past Kirita to the closet by the bed. The door had a decorative pattern of holes that also served as ventilation. I opened it up and, sure enough, I found a little camera staring back at me.

"I've decided to get at you from a different angle altogether."

In the past, I used to interact with suspects in all kinds of ways, whatever it took to arrest them. But not anymore. I didn't have it in me.

My phone buzzed. It was one of my "sources" from the underworld. A detective's work relies on such connections. To reach into the darkness, you need to know the rules.

—*I found a video that has the guy you mentioned, Kazunari Yoshikawa. Pretty obscure stuff.*

"Send it over."

—*Okay. I'll warn you though . . . it's hard to watch. This guy's messed up.*

3

There they were, on a gigantic screen, Kazunari Yoshikawa and Ami Ito.

I was sitting with the owner of the fetish club, the one who had been questioned by Togashi and Ichioka. I asked if he would watch the video with me and comment on Yoshikawa's style. Acting cordial, the owner said it was good timing, since he had a multimedia event the next day and had already set up a screen, but as our viewing party went on, his expression grew more and more tense.

"This video was put out by an independent adult video producer."

The owner nodded at my explanation.

"Evidently, Yoshikawa told their buyer something odd . . . Went on about how rope gets tangled on its own. How if you leave a piece of rope alone, it naturally gets tangled up in knots you never tied . . . This happens with electrical cords for sure. If you put a bunch of string into a box with a dowel or what have you, the string naturally wraps itself around it . . . because of how it's made. He said that rope does the same thing . . . Does that make sense to you?"

The first scene was derivative, nothing special. Using a vibrator, Yoshikawa penetrated Ami Ito, who was tied up. The content was erotic, but Yoshikawa and Ito looked apathetic. Like they were only doing this because they had to.

What gave me pause was the second scene.

Yoshikawa passed a rope around Ami Ito's body. Carelessly, no sense of form. It was a sloppy mess. As if he thought the rope could tie itself, or wrap itself around her, naturally. Next, he passed the loose end over a rod suspended from the ceiling and pulled hard, giving it all his weight, hoisting Ami Ito up into the air.

Ropes dug randomly into her muscles. Ami floated in midair at a perilous angle. She let out a painful cry. Her slender body was being squeezed with awesome force. Yoshikawa, holding the rope, had a blank look on his face, but even so, he looked like he had something on his mind.

". . . That's not kinbaku," said the owner, anger in his voice. "What the hell . . . This guy is nuts . . . He's unbelievable."

". . . I'd agree that this is different. I've seen it once before, in person."

Unable to conceal his anger, the owner kicked his drink back.

"I'm by no means a connoisseur," I continued, "but one time, I saw a show put on by a renowned rope artist, so famous that he has a following overseas. He worked carefully and briskly, tying up a gorgeous woman dressed in a kimono . . . As the ropes encircled her, she looked a little sad, or maybe distressed. Once she was tied up, the rope artist pulled down her kimono, until her shoulders, collarbones and chest were bare. This made the woman writhe in shame and glare at him for exposing her in front of all these people. Every set of eyes in the whole audience was focused on her body . . . When her body was finally suspended, a wave of fear passed through her, but she had the utmost trust in the rope artist's work and let her body sink into the knots. Gradually, her labored breathing became audible beneath the music . . . The rope artist had barely touched her. He had tied her up as if he were embracing or caressing her with rope. Transported to a faraway place, the woman started to cry. But she didn't go to pieces. She maintained her composure. I'm sure that she was crying from the pain, or the constraint, but there was more to it than that. Crying can leave you feeling refreshed. It was almost like being restrained was helping her let something go. There was a sense of bravery, like she was ready to take even more rope, and maybe bitterness, or even intimacy, towards this man who she had given up her body to, but also joy, or thankfulness, that somebody would pay so much attention to her . . . It wasn't just one feeling. In that sense, it was love."

The owner was still glowering at the video of Yoshikawa.

"That woman was the center of attention. She was the one being held captive, but the audience gazed up at her with rapturous attention. How can I put this? It was a strange reversal. There were about forty people in the black box theater, but over half of them were crying . . . Once it was over, the rope artist untied her right away. Wanting her to feel relieved, in another gesture of love . . . and after that, she threw her arms around him, crying, and he took her in . . . I was floored."

The owner turned his gaze on me. Hard to say if he empathized with my perspective.

"Here's the thing," he said. "The same way a term like BDSM can mean all kinds of things, there are all kinds of different ways of using rope in kinbaku . . . It sounds like what you saw was what we call rope torture . . . We talk about rope artists like they're maestros, or the ones in charge, but the real star of the show is the woman being tied up. Her skill can make or break the whole performance . . . These guys have to be pretty modest types, but their art depends on drawing out what makes these women shine. Nobody needs a rope artist who thinks the whole show is about him. The rope artist is only playing a supporting role . . . but this guy? I have no idea. It's not him or the woman in the spotlight . . . but the ropes. He's obsessed. I've heard him say the ropes were in charge, but I didn't know it was this bad."

The video ended. Once again, the screen went blank.

". . . Unless an artist's style blatantly resembles someone else's, it's pretty tough to guess who was his teacher . . . There's a decent chance that he learned everything from going to shows or watching videos. One thing I'll say for sure, though, is that this guy loves his Shinto rites."

No doubt about that. Yoshikawa's choice of costumery was almost like something a Shinto priest would wear, while the horizontal rod was vaguely reminiscent of the torii gates that mark the entrance of a shrine. There was even a crude bird statue in the background. Birds played a major role in bringing cannabis to Japan.

Birds . . . When Yoshikawa was found dead, his hair was short, but in the video it was long. If he was this immersed in historical rites, there was a possibility that the old scars on his thighs were self-inflicted markings of some kind. When we found him dead, his legs were folded under him. What could that mean?

"Hold on," the owner said. "Based on his costume and the gestures that he makes in the beginning, he does remind me of this other artist . . . not someone very famous, but a specific rope artist for sure. I actually think I heard he passed away . . . Give me a second."

The owner turned to his computer. A few clicks later, he sighed, not finding what he wanted, but got up and fetched an external hard drive from a room out back. His long fingers clicked the buttons of the mouse and keyboard, searching the files. At length, a video of a kinbaku performance filled the screen. It was a low-quality recording of a live show at some club somewhere, but it was clear that this performance drew from Shinto imagery as well.

"So this artist . . . huh?" the owner said.

For an instant, the woman being tied up looked just like Ami Ito. But something was off. The man tying her up was some old guy I'd never seen before.

"That's weird," the owner said. "She looks just like the woman from the last one . . . but she's not."

I'd thought the same thing as the owner, when I saw her on the screen.

"It isn't her," he said. "This isn't the same girl."

Was she an Ami Ito lookalike? My heart was thumping. This made no sense.

4

I brought my parched lips to the glass of whisky and leaned into the counter.

What was that song? Some up-tempo piano number, played by a jazz trio. It sounded so familiar, but they didn't name the song or the group when it was over.

". . . Here you are."

The bartender set down my croque monsieur. Not actually on the menu. I'd imposed.

"Wish we could do better . . . That's white bread from the supermarket next door."

"Please. You'll spoil it."

I wouldn't say that they should add it to the menu, but it was comforting.

She'd looked just like Ami Ito. Though nobody would have confused them for sisters. Could it be they only looked alike because of the poor resolution? If they stood together, side by side, perhaps the difference would be clear.

It sounded like the rope artist was long gone, but one of his students was alive. If a detective like me knocked on his door, he'd probably freeze up. So I asked the owner of the fetish club to introduce us. No word yet.

". . . In the midst of an investigation?"

"Hmm? Yeah."

"This one doesn't sound too thrilling."

I trained my eyes on the bartender. He was just shy of sixty, but he looked as young as ever.

"I'm not in this line of work for thrills."

"Sure," he said, giving me that grin of his. "Then what about that one a while back? You were practically walking on air . . . though I'm not sure that was healthy."

As time goes by, I've closed myself off. In a sense, I'm more and more myself. I've lost interest in being social and my favorite things can fit on a short list. The sort of jazz they played here, classic rock. Croque monsieurs and cheesesteak. Plain miso soup, made from white miso, with nothing in it. Basement-level bars. Mechanical clocks. I stopped going to movies once they made them all nonsmoking, but sometimes I'll pop in a DVD. Now and then I'll read a novel. Though I only spend my time on a handful of writers and directors. That my taste in clothes has changed from what it used to be perhaps shows the extent of my boredom. It feels good wearing things that are a bit out of the ordinary.

It's hard to say if I enjoy detective work. Though once

upon a time, I felt its pull. I derived satisfaction from developing relationships with criminals, then reeling in the net. From the bewilderment or terror in the expression of a suspect. From the feeling of knowing I could book them anytime I wanted, but still putting it off a little longer, savoring the moment. Over the years, these pleasures have gradually faded into nothing. What's changed? Too many things to count.

I could feel myself getting depressed. On the verge of some kind of recollection, I redirected my attention. I wasn't here to baste in my own juices.

"My memory's been failing me," said the bartender. I guess something in my face had asked him for commiseration. He paused the conversation to put in a new CD. One time, he had apologized to me for not playing jazz on vinyl, though I wasn't complaining. I had no preference for vinyl.

"I'll see a face I know I've seen before, then try to place it, but when I finally do, I'll remember that this person and I had a terrible experience . . . It makes me wish my memory was even worse."

Faintly but distinctly, I could hear Togashi laughing at me in the forest like a madman. He had an anxious personality, but I'm not sure that he realized how much other people influenced his well-being.

Some people see anxiety as a personal failing. Maybe they're callous or coldhearted. Or maybe they lack the strength required to make space for another person's hardships. Togashi had plenty of shortcomings, same as me, but at least he didn't run around insulting people.

I'd made no effort to get closer to the man, but I can't say that I hated him.

I was waiting for the owner of the fetish club to get back to me. But when I checked my phone, I had a missed call from Maiko Kirita. I called her back. The call had been from thirty minutes earlier. Around the time that I had come into the bar. How could I have missed it?

It rang on her end seven times before she picked up.

". . . What's up?"

"Sorry . . . I tried hanging up before it went through, but I guess it went through anyway."

"What's wrong?." I was about to take a sip of whisky, but I stopped. "Are you crying?"

"I'm sorry. I can't do this anymore."

That was it. She hung up. I called her back, but she didn't answer.

5

The woman who came through the door stepped by me and took off her clothes.

She looked like Ami Ito, only younger. She was an acquaintance of a student of the old rope artist from the video, now dead. The owner of the fetish club worked quickly. Once we had picked a time, he sent the name of a love hotel where she would meet me. It may come as a surprise to some, but most people in that industry mean business.

". . . Stop right there."

The woman stopped.

"I'm a detective. Here to talk."

The woman stared at me. She looked ready to run, but she sat down on the bed.

". . . Think I could have a cigarette?"

She was pretty relaxed, for someone sitting down with a detective. She lit the cigarette I gave her using her own lighter. Down below she wore a navy skirt, but from the waist up she was half undressed, in a blue brassiere.

Something about her reminded me of Maiko Kirita, even though she didn't smoke cigarettes. I'd called her one more time, on my way here. That time, Kirita picked up. She talked to me like everything was fine. Almost cheerful. I was confused. Sweeping these conflicting bits of information from my mind, I focused on the woman there in front of me.

". . . Just to make sure, but you aren't Ami Ito, right? What's your name?"

". . . Mari Yamamoto."

The woman didn't look away from me.

"Do you know the man in this photograph? Kazunari Yoshikawa. That's Ami Ito there, beside him. You look a lot alike . . . don't you think?"

"I've never seen this guy before, and I don't know her either . . . What's the idea? I told the other detective the same thing."

The other detective? Had Togashi beat me to her? When I showed her a photograph of him, she confirmed my suspicion.

"What did this man do with you?"

"The exact same thing. He showed me the photo of those two and asked me if I knew them. I said no . . . He kept on saying I was Ami Ito. I told him that I wasn't, but he wouldn't believe me."

"Anything else?"

"He fell asleep."

"Asleep?"

"Yeah, crying as he nodded off. He talked a little more . . . but then he fell asleep again. So I went home . . . Why bother asking me the same things, after him?"

I lit a cigarette myself. Steadying my breath.

"Because he's dead."

"Huh?"

"It was a suicide. Though if you ask me, he was murdered."

The last time that I saw Togashi, he couldn't keep his hand out of his pocket. He must have been gripping a pistol. But there was no way we were going to have a shootout. He would need to put some distance between us for him to use it.

The woman's face went tense, but she soon relaxed. Way too quickly. She looked away from me, setting her eyes on the middle distance. On a place that wasn't here.

"Is that so . . . I wish I'd helped him out."

"Huh?"

"He was a worried guy, you know? Carrying a lot around . . . I wish I could've helped him let some of it go."

Blue light, unabashedly distasteful, bathed the woman.

". . . Do you have something to tell me?"

"It was just a feeling that I got . . . I get it from you too."

I had been glancing at her, but I looked away and grabbed her clothes and tossed them on the bed. She showed no sign of getting dressed.

"You could've been killed, too, you know."

". . . You don't say."

"As far as the official record is concerned, Kazunari Yoshikawa has been murdered, and Ami Ito, the top suspect, is at large. Even though Ami Ito has been dead for months. But what do you think would happen if a woman like you, who looks just like Ami Ito, wrote a suicide note and killed herself in some hotel somewhere? This whole thing would be over. If Togashi had been a different kind of person, you'd be dead."

Looking at her, I felt the same thing that I felt with Kirita. She was beautiful. Though no part of me wanted to have her to myself. I had lost that impulse long ago. Since losing Kyoko—no, if only it had been that easy.

"Want to know the real reason I went home?" she asked.

Mari Yamamoto looked at me.

"After he fell asleep again, I heard him muttering 'I can't kill her.' I had no way of knowing who he meant, but I didn't want to take a chance. What really creeped me out was this planner that he showed me . . . Someone had written down the name of the club where I work."

"Was the handwriting like this?"

I showed her a sample of Togashi's writing. The characters leaned to one side in a memorable way.

"No, I don't think so. It was messy. Like it was written by a kid."

". . . You should get away while you can."

"Why is that?"

"If this investigation goes any further, you're liable to get pulled into it again. And this time, I think it's likely you'll be blamed for something big. Show me your phone."

She handed it to me. Almost too obediently. Not a smartphone, but the kind that folds in half.

"I don't care how old it is, it's not supposed to be this thick."

I whacked the old phone on the desk. The back part of the case popped off, and a tiny GPS transmitter fell onto the carpet. It had been tacked on using tape.

"They've been tracking your location this whole time. Though maybe you've realized that by now."

〰〰〰〰〰〰〰

WE GOT INTO the car. Mari Yamamoto got into the passenger's seat, no sign of trepidation. Her eyes were locked on me. A little too obediently.

"I have a hard time with wide-open spaces," she told me in a languid voice. "So sometimes, I'll just grab a cab."

I left the GPS transmitter in the room. It was possible someone might come looking for her. I knew it was excessive, but I called the precinct just in case and asked for them to have somebody keep an eye out.

"That's you, right?"

I handed her a tablet and showed her the video. The

one of her being tied up by the old rope artist, now dead. I stepped on the gas. First things first, we had to leave this place behind.

". . . Yeah, this is me."

"What do you think of this one?"

It was the second of the two scenes featuring Kazunari Yoshikawa. The one where Ami Ito, tied up in his careless knots, gets suspended in the air. Her shrieking voice rang through the car. A cry that could be read as either agony or joy.

". . . I've done this sort of thing before."

"You have?"

"Yeah. Or, someone did this to me once. I was shocked . . . it was totally different from normal kinbaku. I was blindfolded at the time, so I have no idea who he was."

There was a strong chance it was Yoshikawa.

"While I was tied up, the rope artist kept saying this weird thing to me, in an excited voice. 'You would be the ideal offering.' Isn't that weird?"

". . . Offering?"

"He said that haniwa were a disgrace, but that the clothes were not enough. I have no idea what he meant by that . . . but it freaked me out."

Haniwa were a disgrace. But the clothes were not enough.

"He said that?"

"Yes."

I pulled the car onto the shoulder and called Ichioka.

"Do you know where Ami Ito was buried? She had no family, right?"

—*Whoa, hold your horses.*

"It's fine, just tell me."

Ichioka looked into her file and told me where to find her grave. It was a temple plot. As soon as the map opened on my phone, I decided. We were going. It was a little far from here, across the prefecture, but I spun the wheel at the next light and turned the car around.

"Hey . . . have you had plastic surgery?"

"Yep."

"Who asked you to do that?"

". . . I can't tell you."

I pressed the pedal to the floor. Even racing, though, we might not make it there today.

"Why?"

"It would cost me my life. Still . . ."

"What?"

"Maybe it doesn't matter anymore."

Her whole body went lax as she sank into the seat. Like she was gazing up at something, but the only thing above her was the roof of the car: the roof of an E-Class Mercedes-Benz, emblematic of our consumer society. The roof of the car that I bought from a friend a while back, somewhat begrudgingly, knowing it was a bad look for a detective. A roof that I was sick of looking at as well.

I had a hunch it wouldn't be long before I met this person that she couldn't tell me about. I got the sense that we were similar.

"How did you and Togashi meet?"

"I'm a prostitute. My boss told me which hotel to go to, so I went. And he was there."

"I assume this boss of yours is also the one who ordered you to make that video we watched and had Yoshikawa tie you up. How does he communicate with you?"

"I get a text from the manager of the escort agency I work for. The boss only ever contacts me via the manager, I never hear from him directly . . . That time, he told me to meet someone at a hotel, but there was something weird about the way he phrased it. He also wanted me to give the man that I was meeting an address, but before I could, he fell asleep again, so I wrote it in his planner. Not like I had a clue . . . Nobody told me why he had to know this address, but I didn't want to get myself in trouble, so I wrote it in the planner and went home."

"What kind of address are we talking about?"

She gave the address to the best of her ability. As far as I could tell, it was the pond, not far from where I found him walking.

". . . What's weird is that a few days ago, the manager stopped responding. And then yesterday, the texts I sent him started bouncing. This is just a guess, but I bet if you looked into it, his name wouldn't be linked to the account

. . . I've obviously met his boss, our boss, before . . . since he's in charge of me, but I don't know his name, or where he lives. I guess I haven't seen him for a year now. One thing about him stands out."

She took a short breath. For a while now, her voice had been trembling.

"He's missing a finger . . . the middle one."

His middle finger? I scanned my memory. I didn't know someone like that, not on this case anyway. The owner of the fetish club had all his digits. And it obviously wasn't Maiko Kirita. The man at the escort agency who said he was in charge and vouched for her was a young blond guy with a nice build and all his fingers.

"So why the plastic surgery?"

"I don't know . . . I met my boss back when I was going from one sex club to another. When he saw my face, he got worked up and told me, in this kind of panicked voice, that I was bad luck. He called the place where I was working and had me taken off the roster. Then he brought me to a plastic surgeon, who changed the shape of my face over multiple sessions, and made the bridge of my nose higher. I had to change my hair and eyebrows and my clothes too. But he didn't seem satisfied . . . for a while after that, he basically owned me . . . and strictly speaking, he still does."

This final comment sounded too sincere. It was hard to tell how much I could trust her. Though she seemed plenty puzzled by her own sincerity. She looked like she was going to cry. Out came the tears.

". . . I don't know. Maybe I've finally hit my limit."

Her voice hadn't changed in the slightest, but tears were streaming from her eyes.

"And here I'd thought I'd hit my limit ages ago . . . Women in this line of work have to decide in one look whether a person's above us or below us. The same as dogs do. We need to figure out who's in control. I wonder about you," she said.

Still crying.

"Can you save me?"

6

We checked into a business hotel. The twin room was spacious, but a little old. A layer of dust clung to a desk lamp with a twisted neck and to the pleated edges of the curtains. From the outside, it had looked far more desirable.

"It's kind of . . . gross," said Yamamoto. There was a dark stain on the fabric of one of the headboards.

"Just a guess," I said, "but I bet some guy who watches too much porn tried to finish on a girl's face, only she dodged it."

"Oh . . . you think so?"

"Who knows, right?"

I couldn't help admiring this unknown woman for her skillful dodge.

"I've got a long way to go tomorrow, but you should come along. If I were you, for the time being, I'd avoid being alone."

"Okay."

Yamamoto had eaten all the pasta that I bought her at the convenience store. Mildly amused, she watched me sip my miso soup between mouthfuls of my pasta. As I picked all of the solid ingredients from my soup, she looked at me with raised eyebrows.

". . . You must be tired," I said. "Time for bed."

She gave me a puzzled look, but when she realized that I wasn't looking back at her she went to bed. I took a shower and put on a fresh pair of underwear from the convenience store, then put the pair I had been wearing in the plastic bag and tied it off with a tight knot. Donning a bathrobe that was not my style, I had myself a smoke. The woman was asleep. I dimmed the lights. My body temperature was dropping.

What was that sound? I felt a strange pain in my lower back. Purple and blue lights flashed before my eyes, as the pain eventually spread to my legs. I could have sworn I had been on my bed, but I was seated in a chair. My socks slipped off, like magic, and I crawled across the floor, looking around me as I headed for the window. But the window wouldn't budge. This was bad. I had to think. It was locked. Unless I could unlock it, I wasn't getting out the window. It was cold outside. I wasn't sure if going out there was the right decision.

—*Stop worrying.*

It was Kyoko's voice.

—*She's your type. I thought the same thing when you*

visited Kirita. She's great. The two of you were made for each other.

"Cut it out."

I couldn't see her. But the room wasn't too dark to see. The window and the strobing colors had both disappeared.

—Why?

"This is pathetic . . . I've summoned you, with my subconscious. I must be sleeping. What happened to my cigarette?"

—It went out.

I could just barely see the limits of the room, but I was unable to move. Was I still in the chair? Where was my cigarette?

"I know I'm only hearing what I want to hear."

—Didn't I tell you? I may be gone, but that doesn't mean this isn't actually my voice.

"You're dead. It's a fact."

—I may be gone, but it's still my voice you're hearing.

"I don't get it."

—What don't you get? You're wearing prayer beads. That's a pretty fancy suit for a Buddhist. Just saying.

I laughed. Just as I felt a warmth suffusing me, another feeling bubbled up to stop it. Call it a conditioned reflex, engineered to stop the spread of any and all warm feelings. I felt myself flip the switch. The pain was getting worse. Though perhaps it was appropriate. I heard the sound of breathing. Whose? Oh yeah, this was—

I felt myself reentering my body, seated in the chair. The room was the same as before, though something had changed in my perspective. Ensconced in darkness, I was wide awake. I could hear Yamamoto breathing. She was in bed, fast asleep.

". . . Ah, ahhh."

What? I looked over at her bed. I realized I'd been hearing her cry out like this the whole time I was dreaming.

"Stop, ah, ah."

Her body writhed under the covers.

"No, please, no, ahhh!"

She was exhausted, motionless. But then I heard her voice again, this time more softly.

"Ah, ah . . ."

"You all right over there?"

She muttered something and attempted to sit up, but she lost control and flopped back down on the bed. Regarding me with terror in her eyes, she heaved her shoulders as she breathed and touched her cheeks. She was sweating. She had sweated a lot already.

". . . It was a nightmare. Want something to drink?"

". . . No."

"I'm going to bed. Early day tomorrow."

I got into my own bed. But she sat up in hers.

"I told you how that man basically owns me."

". . . Yeah."

"He broke me in . . . so I would cum more easily . . . Um, are you okay with talking about this?"

"Huh?"

"Lately I keep finding myself in the company of people who shut down or lash out when they hear something that falls outside of their experience . . . I can tell that you're not like that, but I had to ask."

". . . It's fine."

Stretched out, I turned to face her bed. I realized that she'd had her eyes on me for this entire time. The dimmed lights cast an amber glow over her body. Through a cascade of dust. The particles almost looked like sentient beings. The countless dead, gathering around us for a lusty tale.

". . . For a long, long time, he had his way with me . . . One of his favorite things was to use me for a footrest. Like when he sat at his computer, to do work. He kept me on a leash made from a rope tied in a loop around my neck. People came to see him. They were shocked. First they saw him, no surprise, but then they saw this woman cowering at his feet, totally naked, on a leash. He reminded me to make eye contact with the guests. If one of them looked down on me, like I was trash, I got so excited I could barely stand it. This feeling of mounting pleasure traveled through me. When I was like that, if he kicked me with his heel, like just below the hip, or near my pubic bone . . . it made me cum . . . I know it sounds hard to believe."

"No . . . I know someone like that. I've heard of this."

"It's sort of a conditioned reflex . . . one thing connects to another thing, even though they're unrelated. It's second nature, so you cum almost automatically. Under the right circumstances, some women can cum with a flick of the whip. It's different for me, but all some women need is a certain look, or word, or a slight touch to make them cum . . . although not anyone can make it happen. There needs to be a preexisting relationship for it to work. With someone you'd kneel down to, unconditionally . . . Women in my line of work have extremely strong preferences. If a gross guy forces himself onto me, I'll push back like my life depends on it. But if my boss tells me to do it, the sex will make me cum, no matter how gross the guy is . . . Does that make sense?"

The dust cascaded through the room. All at once, her face was young. Remembering these things was not unsettling for her. Her eyes glistened in the dark as she experienced desire with an expression that retained an air of childhood. Eyes ready to abandon everything. All the trappings of society. A face ready to give up the past, the self, and everything there was, to be a kid again.

"Then, he told me it was time that I got dirtier . . . Go out and make yourself real dirty, he said, don't come back till you're a pig. He would barely look at me . . . I told you that he doesn't have his middle finger, right?"

". . . Yeah."

"Right, so then, he starts staring at his finger, like it was bothering him. What's this, he said. I was tied up on the bed. He had made me cum multiple times. I could feel this clustering sensation, deep inside of me, as if what we had just done was still happening. I could have cum again, at any time. My body was extremely sensitive . . . but then, he pricked the knuckle of his middle finger with a knife."

The dust churned, sweeping through the air.

"Then, screaming like crazy, he cut into the skin. Everything was red with blood. I was so scared I was shivering, but he was really riled up. I hadn't seen his face look so alive in a long time. 'Look, my finger's gone,' he told me. 'See? Isn't there. I wonder where it went?' I was in a daze, but when I saw his face, scared as I was, I wanted him, and touched myself with my own fingers, half-unconsciously. Maybe I was just trying to soothe myself. But then he looked me right in the eye, really staring at me, as hard as he could possibly stare, and said, 'I'll be inside of you forever. Wherever you go now, whoever you're with, whatever you do, my middle finger will be deep inside your pussy. Flicking at the nastiest parts of you whenever you remember that it's there. For the rest of your life, my finger will be thrust into the most sensitive part of you, stroking you passionately, wildly. At every serious event, and every time you fall in love, and at the funerals for both your parents, it'll twitch inside your pussy, so that you're constantly reminded of the kind of woman that you are. A landscape of fresh blood at your back.'"

The woman took a deep breath. Shivering all over.

"Could you get me . . . some water?"

I got out of bed and grabbed a bottle of water from the fridge. But she wouldn't take it from me.

". . . Is that what the nightmare was about? The finger."

"No. That happens all the time. But this time, it was something else."

She looked away.

"I was doing it with you."

I steadied my breath, making sure she wouldn't notice. Then I lit another cigarette.

"What he did, it was almost like hypnosis or something. Of course, it didn't work exactly how he wanted. It's not like I actually feel his finger inside me all the time. But I'll admit, sometimes I think about it . . . Something great will happen to me, and I'll feel it moving, a reminder of the kind of woman that I am . . . This sort of thing can happen while I'm sleeping, too. In the depths of my subconscious, I'll see his finger, floating in the dark. Whatever I'm dreaming morphs into a sex dream. Suddenly, I'm doing it with somebody. Only inside of me . . . The sort of men who sleep with me, they like it rough. They do it hard, so that it hurts. They think I like it like that. But they're wrong. I only enjoy pain from the right person. If a stranger hurts me, it just hurts. But when I was with you, in the dream . . . you were so sweet to me."

I smoked my cigarette. I felt like it was me who had been dreaming. Though what kind of a dream it was, I couldn't say.

"Most of the time, with sex, I'm getting tossed around, so I barely feel a thing. It's like I turn into a thing and wait for it to end. But with you, it was so sweet. I've been treated like a thing by lots of men. But you were sweet, the way you kissed me, the way you touched my breasts, and how you moved your lips across my neck, and sucked my nipples . . . I resisted you. Told you to stop. Because I knew if you were sweet like that, I'd feel it all. But you kept going . . . It felt like I was being raped. Even though you were so gentle . . . I forgot about the finger."

She was upright in bed, making eyes at me through the dark. Again I tried to steady out my breath.

"I think you're beautiful. I'd love to sleep with you. But it's no use."

The cataracts of dust fell away. As if no longer interested.

". . . How come?"

"Because I'm done getting mixed up in people's lives."

I went over to her bed and took her head into my arm. I hugged it gently. The heat of her body made me realize just how much I wanted her. As I tamped this feeling into nothing, I smiled a joyless smile.

". . . That's enough for tonight."

"You're so . . ."

"I'm not fond of analysis."

"Still."

"I'll tell you one thing, though." I grinned. Stroking her gently as I spoke. "I've killed a lot of people in my time."

7

As we ascended the stone staircase, I looked up at the gray torii ahead of us.

Mari Yamamoto had tacitly agreed to come along. The shrine was on the smaller side, overgrown with grass and trees, a lonesome place with no one else around. Beyond the torii was a perfectly straight path of flagstones leading to the center of the shrine. Some of the stones were chipped, and they were mostly covered up with gritty dirt, but none was even the slightest bit askew. The wind blew faintly, through a silence so profound it even muted out the smells of vegetation.

The two of us passed through the torii.

A FEW YEARS back, I drove a suspect to suicide.

He had raped and subsequently killed a female nurse, and I had proof. Her fiancé begged me, "Kill him, he's a murderer." Said it with a blank look on his face. "I'm begging you. He needs to die." The murdered nurse, his partner, had been pregnant.

A single-victim homicide rarely results in capital punishment in Japan. I led the suspect to believe that I was covering for him and met with him each day. I talked about how good a person the dead nurse had been, how sincerely her fiancé had awaited the arrival of their unborn child. Some of what I said was made-up. I began to weave a story and told it to the people in his circle. I pretended I was going to prove his innocence, that I was on the trail of someone else. I led him to believe that whether or not he was arrested would come down to how well I finagled things. The suspect had always been unstable, a fool who lacked the callousness required to accomplish evil deeds. The day that he confessed to me, in tears, I told him I was having none of it. "What are you saying?" I asked. "There's no way you could have done it. Imagine what was going through the criminal's mind . . ."

Sometimes I set up a dynamic where it's almost like I'm a psychiatrist consulting with a patient. The suspect and I delve into the matrix of the setup. What's another way to say it? Maybe it's like being a fortune teller who latches onto someone famous and destroys their life. Or an unsavory recruiter for a small-scale cult. But it wasn't my intention for this man to kill himself. Things didn't go as planned. The idea was to make him suffer constantly. To prod him into a chaotic darkness, a psychological penumbra from which he had no hope of reemerging.

When it came to light that he had committed suicide, the bereaved fiancé was left without a sense of liberation or accomplishment, although his wish had essentially been granted. I can't say I was very surprised. It's almost a cliche, but killing the criminal won't bring the woman or the child in her belly back to life. The fiancé had been born with a weak constitution, always in and out of hospitals. He had been on the mend, but he was dead two years after the perpetrator killed himself.

What made me do these things? Had I been trying to live out the obsessions that were haunting the fiancé? Or did I derive some pleasure from inserting the suspect into the matrix I created, just to drive him crazy? Whatever used to draw me to this work has disappeared. I've long since given up. My habits got the better of me. I got roped into a battle between gangsters armed with guns and killed two people. But that's not all. There's more. Thanks to repeated instances of acting out of line, I had been forced to step down from the first division. But I was able to forgive myself. I had grown tired. Of everything. Case in point, I had declined to start something with Maiko Kirita.

"WHAT'S HERE . . ." Yamamoto asked me.

"Haniwa and clothes."

"... Haniwa?"

She turned to me.

"Yoshikawa called you an offering. *He said that haniwa were a disgrace, but the clothes were not enough* ... Long ago, when a member of the Japanese imperial family died, civilians were buried alive—*as offerings*—to accompany them in their graves. To replace this brutal practice, clay figurines called haniwa were buried as a *substitute*. There was very little clothing in the apartment where Yoshikawa's body was discovered, and none of it was Ito's style. The way I see it, he did something with Ami's clothes, as a memorial to her. Since he said haniwa were a disgrace, and that the clothes were not enough, we can deduce that the clothes were buried. Ami Ito's body, meanwhile, was interred at the temple. Judging from the map, that temple is right over there, next to this shrine. It's common for shrines and temples to be neighbors. This shrine is one of many dedicated to the Inbe clan, as if I wasn't sure this was the place already. They were a powerful family in antiquity, tasked by the imperial court with the administration of religious rites that made ceremonial use of the cannabis plant, but they were defeated in a power struggle and pushed off the stage of history ... None of that happened here, of course, but it does mean that this shrine has strong links to mythology. We know that Yoshikawa had an affinity for Shinto ... and that Ami Ito was buried at the temple over there. We have no way of knowing what his mental state was at the time, but there is reason to believe that Yoshikawa buried the clothes here, on the grounds of the shrine. And perhaps made another offering while he was at it."

THINGS WERE INTERESTING with Kyoko. We were together for six years, but we never married or moved in together. Try as I might, I couldn't give her what she needed. In contrast to my hopelessly warped personality, she was almost too good of a person. A sincere woman who could watch the sort of cheesy TV shows that I thought were useless trash like she was in a dream.

I remember seeing this funny caption on a show once, just before it jumped to a commercial.

Next up, an act that's been topping charts for years!

I never watched TV, and if I walked into the room and saw a gag like this, it rankled me enough to switch it off. But not this time. "Topping the charts for years?" Kyoko said. "Think it's the guy who sang 'Freeze My Heart'?"

"Freeze My Heart" was an old enka song performed by a dead-serious singer who had not exactly topped the charts. And yet, for whatever the reason, I thought she might be right. Takes me back, I told myself. That was a great song, maybe I'll put it on today.

The commercial break was over. The show welcomed the band Dreams Come True. Of course. I was a fool for thinking that a dead-serious enka singer was going to appear on stage and sing a sad song for the crowd.

". . . You're crazy, know that?" I said, cracking up. It made Kyoko laugh too. "What made you think of that old song anyway?"

From time to time, I felt myself get wrapped up in her thoughts. She had a strange habit of referring to the contents of her pockets or her bag as "items." One time, during a search, I accidentally told a suspect "Put those items of yours, uh . . ." but was unable to complete the sentence. When she was diagnosed with cancer at age thirty-five, and we learned it had metastasized to the point where she could not be saved, I decided that this world we live in makes no sense. There was nothing normal about a world where a woman like her could just die, out of nowhere, in her thirties. No army of happy people can make up for that kind of senselessness.

"Not exactly good news," Kyoko said. "I just hope it doesn't hurt."

She had lost most of her hair. That's what chemo does to you.

Sitting beside her hospital bed, I wiped away her tears with my fingertips, saying that I wished I could have given her what she needed, that I wished I could have made her happy. I had been taking up space in her life, at the age when women have to face the question of marriage.

"Don't be silly," she said. "I was happy."

Then she rattled off a list of memories, frivolous moments that we'd shared. Like how I claimed that sitting underneath the kotatsu went against my sensibilities, but looked so happy when I actually tried it. Or the time I went with her to Hawaii, despite repeatedly insisting that I hated crowded places, and was grumpy the whole trip, but came home so thoroughly sunburned that I looked like I had learned my lesson. Or the first time we had sex. Or the way that I consoled her about tough stuff at work. Christmas. New Year's. Tasty restaurants. Books she read. Destinations. Fun concerts.

Marriage and family . . . As it turned out, I was the one who cared what people thought of us. She let herself be happy and enjoyed life to the fullest. She was still telling me how happy she had been when she died at thirty-six. Hospitalized the last year of her life.

"How many times do I need to tell you? I don't care if we have the same name or not. That's never been important to me."

And yet I blamed myself. For what, though? Taking up space in her life? Wanting to be with her? Being unable to change the way I am? Not trying to change? Not even after she was gone? At this point, I can't say what I blame myself for having done.

The world we live in makes no sense. What's sensible about a world where a woman like Kyoko dies, out of nowhere, at age thirty-six?

I used to dream of Kyoko all the time. But at this point, it's been years. Or, actually, it's possible I still do, but forget it all the second I wake up.

"As soon as I'm gone, find someone else to love . . . Though hearing myself say this, I doubt you'll let it happen," she told me, smiling through the pain.

"Yeah. Not happening."

"You should really love somebody else, though. You're so lovable."

I LOOKED OVER my shoulder at the dusty torii we had passed through.

At the main shrine, I dropped a handful of coins into the offertory box, without stopping to pray, and had a walk around. Mari Yamamoto didn't pray either. Though some shrines are a place to venerate the emperor, they run the gamut, some dedicated to mythological personages or old families in the area, while others have a more animistic orientation. Some even celebrate material wealth.

"I thought there would be something here that would have lured Yoshikawa, but maybe I was wrong. Let's head to Ami Ito's grave. Although . . . we haven't seen the inside of this old shrine. Not like we can, you know . . ."

"It doesn't matter if you don't believe, we can't just peek behind the door."

The wind picked up. We could see the rows of stone

graves on the temple grounds. Someday we're all reduced to bone and disappear.

"Should we contact the chief priest?"

The land behind the shrine was overgrown. On a tall frond of grass, someone had tied a strip of paper. Blue.

It took me a few seconds after seeing it to realize what it was.

". . . Looks like someone has been through here."

"Huh? I don't see anything."

"Look closely, at the way the grass falls. Very subtle."

An unruly wood, in stark contrast to the rows of graves. Upon closer examination, the thin strip of blue paper had been tied to the tall grass in a messy knot. Of course it was blue. Yoshikawa wouldn't have it any other way. I forged ahead. The stomped-down grass had mostly righted itself, but a vague path could be seen. I followed it. Screened by tall grasses, the tip of another blue strip of paper was barely visible ahead. I went closer.

Then I found it. Four stakes of bamboo, skinny ones, thrust into the ground. Ropes were strung from stake to stake, forming a peculiar square, while paper strips of white and blue hung from the ropes.

". . . What's this?" asked Mari Yamamoto. "Gives me the creeps."

I kicked the stakes down.

"Whoa, isn't that a little much?"

". . . This isn't the doing of the shrine. At first glance, it may look like some kind of sacred Shinto space, but the knots are all wrong . . . Look. The rope is wrapped around the bamboo, *almost like it grew there naturally*. They don't tie knots like this in Shinto. They do tie strips of white paper to rope, but these are white and blue. At some point Yoshikawa cut off his long hair. He had those old scars on his thighs, right? That was an ancient Eurasian custom. So was a preference for the color blue. Another ancient Eurasian custom. Yoshikawa has to be responsible for this . . . I'll bet there's something buried here."

In the square zone, marked off by the ropes, the grass had only grown back a few inches.

". . . Alright, start digging."

"No way. Why can't you do it yourself?"

". . . I don't want my suit getting dirty. Or my watch. They're expensive."

"Unbelievable. You're scaring me. Do it yourself . . ."

"What if there's some kind of bacteria in the dirt? That'd be awful."

"What? How is it any different for me?"

—*There's nothing there.*

I spun around and saw a man a fair distance away. Just after I had felt his presence, behind me to the right.

"Who are you?"

"The chief priest . . . of the shrine."

So he was alive. Without a doubt, it was the old man from the video, who we had reason to believe had influenced Yoshikawa. The same rope artist who had tied up Yamamoto. He said he was the chief priest, but he was wearing jeans and a green jacket. There were no graves at the shrine. It stood to reason why he would have buried Ami Ito at the neighboring temple.

"I've seen people going into these woods. On the same path as that man . . . I knew this day would come eventually. Ever since I saw that he had died on the news, I've been having awful dreams . . . I'm glad you're here. I take it you're with the police? You don't exactly look it, though."

The chief priest smiled wanly. But when he looked at Yamamoto, there beside me, he was so surprised that he went bug-eyed.

"All right, I see what's going on . . . Come on, I live just down the street. I have something to give to you. Something that Yoshikawa put together, with his back against the wall, in lieu of haniwa and other trinkets, as an offering to Ami Ito."

8

The Confessions of
Kazunari Yoshikawa: 1

Looking back, I've always been a sexual person.

I've lived my life thus far convinced that life was
nothing more than an insipid, contrived waste of time.
It goes without saying, but I place the onus not on this
world, but on myself. My only point of access to euphoria
in this life has been sex. Life as I have known it has been
built around this fact.

How is it that I find myself at this dead end? Is there a
reason I wound up here, or no reason at all?

After seven years in college, I dropped out and was hired
full-time by the adult video production company where
I'd been working for a while. It was a tiny company, just
four of us in total. On one of my first projects, I got to
see a kinbaku scene being filmed. It was odd for a puny
company like us, but for once we rented out a studio for

the shoot. This was the first time that I saw kinbaku being done by a professional. I tensed up all over.

Memories of middle school washed over me. A time when I was imprisoned by sexual urges so extreme I thought I might go crazy. One night after the rain had stopped, I was walking by the riverside and came upon a ruined magazine, left open on the ground. There were pictures of women tied up with ropes. The plants which sprouted languidly from the gravel drooped towards the restrained women, as if they couldn't keep their grassy fingers off of them. The pages of the magazine were soggy. Lit by the gentle orange glow of a distant streetlight, the pictures levitated in the darkness. Gazing down at them, I felt my mouth go dry, knowing I was unable to look away. *That's all I have to do*. I remember vividly the way it felt arriving at this realization. *These women can't move, so they can't fight back, I can do anything I want*. Unable to conceal their sensual bodies, the women in the ropes stared at me with looks of suffering and shame. Like they were luring me into hell. Though I have to stress that my fascination with these tied-up women went no further than that. I didn't come away from this with any special interest in rope.

I made it through puberty, became an adult, and, like most men, had intercourse with several different women. I was thankful for these wonderful experiences, but I couldn't help but feel I was unable to drain myself completely. Sex followed my every waking thought. Sex with people I had no business having sex with. Sex with a woman I had never seen before, walking ahead of me on a dark night. Sex with an acquaintance who had shown no interest in that kind of a relationship with me. I thought of criminal acts that you might see in sexy videos but would be hard to come by in real life. It's not like I had a particular fetish or something. My head was a snow globe of unrealistic obsessions.

As far as I was concerned, sex was inherently unrealistic, confined mostly to the realms of the imagination. The sex that I imagined was always rougher than it was in real life. Real life could not surpass the imagination. And the sort of sex that happened in real life, of the real and safe variety, could only set a small part of my mind at ease. If your sexual dynamic with a person is romantic, what we call unromantic sex is off the table. But I think unromantic sex has its own unique appeal. Maybe I'm wrong for seeing it this way.

Living in a veritable deluge of adult videos and other sexualized content, people today unconsciously accept it as a fact, or take for granted, that desiring a lover they don't have to love is part of being human. To state the obvious, you'll probably get turned on if a video of a naked woman pops up on your screen, but that doesn't mean romantic feelings will wash over you. And through habitual reinforcement, this desire becomes something altogether separate. I don't think we can simply blame the deluge of sexual content for this change. Rather, it might well be that this sort of environment is just enabling a tendency that we, as human beings, have always had. The power of our sexual nature has always been in conflict with morality, and the influence of our imagination only increases its sway.

Having sex with a girlfriend, I sometimes indulged in unrealistic fantasies, like imagining her as a stranger, or that she was being pinned down by a group of men, but perhaps because I was too unadventurous to do anything illegal, or pay for sex, or approach someone out of my league, I was always feeling vaguely unsatisfied, though unable to see why.

That said, when I saw kinbaku in person, it sent the blood rushing through my body, to the point where I could actually feel it moving in my veins. I felt the course of my lifetime taking shape. I'm not even exaggerating, if I could have watched myself, across the room, I bet I would have looked pretty bizarre at the time.

A thin woman in her thirties, whose kimono had been pulled down to her waist, lay with her hands tied behind her back. For reasons I can't explain, she wasn't looking at the camera, but at me, with shame and sorrow in her eyes. The rope had been passed over her bare breasts, then under them, pinching them tightly, as if the presence of her womanhood, the fullness of those breasts, were a

crime in and of itself, a disgrace which the ropes empha-
sized and made into a spectacle for all to see. A rope tied
around her ankles had been tossed over a horizontal rod
suspended from the ceiling, with some slack left on the
end, so if you pulled it hard enough, the woman's pale and
shapely legs would go up, inch by inch, into the air. She
had nothing on under her kimono.

"Gah . . ."

She sighed like she was emptying her lungs. Tied up
like that, she was unable to move. As her legs went up,
it exposed her vagina. For all the no-good men to see.
And for the camera, focused on her body. Her vagina was
already wet. Though nobody had laid a finger on her.

For whatever the reason, the woman only looked at
me, for the entire time. As if her defiled body and her
shame were mine alone to see. The earthy braid of hemp
dug deep into her smooth, pale skin. She let out another
breath. It was like watching the dim zones of my sexual
imagination lighting up in front of me. The creaking rope
sounded like it had been wetted by her sweat. My penis
was erect. My mouth went dry.

". . . Want to give it a try?" the rope artist asked me,
during a short break. I must have looked bizarre enough
that he could tell. The director, also my boss, laughed out
loud and said, "Terrific!" He handed me the rope. What
we call rope is made by spinning hemp yarn into clusters
which are wound into a braid. The second I had laid my

hands on the rough fibers of the countless strands of hemp twisted together, I knew I couldn't get enough and ran my fingers and my palms over the line. My fingers found a home in the dips between the spiraled strands, which made the perfect grip. My digits trembled with exhilaration. Now that my desire had been rendered visible, it stretched before my eyes as if embodied. I felt a force that would allow me to do things to women that I could not do with my body alone. I was enthralled by the beauty of its form. The woman stared at me, caught as I was in this trance state. Eventually her gaze traveled to the shameful bulge in my jeans. She was staring at my hard-on. As I approached her, carrying the loose end of the rope, she smiled and turned around for me. Thin bluish veins ran across her gorgeous back. For some reason, my thoughts went to a picture book about hell that I read when I was little. A woman tied to a post, being roasted by the flames. Except instead of the flames, there was me, holding the rope.

I wrapped the rope around her pale, thin wrists, which she had crossed behind her, and then wrapped it once again and pulled. The ropes twisted tight around her, so that she made a little shriek. After that, my memory gets spotty. I do remember realizing she couldn't move. I also can remember this sensation, like the woman and me were connected by the rope, as if I totally possessed her, like my desire had formed into a braid of nerves that had ensnared her. I clung to her and passed the rope once more over her breasts, tying it off behind her. In awe of the creamy color of her skin against the earthy rope. Next thing I knew, I was latched onto her, lips planted on her neck. But the luxuriant heat under my lips is where my memory blacks out. Afterwards, they showed me a short video. Of me trying to go at it from behind, while my boss and the rope artist laughed and held me back. The next thing I knew, I was on the sidelines, drinking a bottle of imported water. In the corner of my eye, I saw a small black hole cut into the wall and the gray wisp of a crumbled spiderweb. The shoot was long since over.

The actress walked over to me, fresh out of the shower, in a bathrobe. She was smiling. There was an air of tenderness.

"I feel bad . . . leaving you hanging like that."

At the time, I still had no idea what I had done.

". . . I hate texting," she said. "Call me."

With that, the two of us began a strange relationship. Her specialty was being tied up, but depending on the gig, she might be asked to do the tying. On multiple occasions, we met up at a cheap love hotel. A large part of my repertoire was picked up from these sessions.

Take the box tie, one of the basics. Using two ropes, you tie the woman's arms in parallel, behind her back.

"When I'm tied up , . . it's like someone is giving me a great big squeeze. I feel released," she said to me, her breath a little ragged. "All of the tension disappears, poof, just like that . . . Even when there's mutual consent, I can't help but feel resistance towards sex. If I'm tied up, though, it's like . . . there's nothing I can do, know what I mean? My resistance falls away. Like I'm free to feel whatever happens, like it's all okay. Because I can't resist, if I'm tied up like that, I'm free to be a different version of myself. That's what I mean by feeling released . . . Ah, ahhh."

The ropes were digging into her white, beautiful skin. I lost my inhibition and mopped my tongue over her body. Losing myself in her.

"And because I can't resist . . . I become powerless. The only choice is to rely on them, rely on you. Sometimes this leads to an almost romantic kind of feeling . . . Since I'm powerless, at their mercy, since I need to keep them happy, it's almost like I give my heart away, completely . . . Know how sometimes, like in a bank robbery or something, a person will start feeling these romantic feelings towards the robber, as a way of hiding from their fear? It's just like that. It goes beyond the physical. Rope links two people, from the spirit. There's nothing quite like being tied up to the point where you can barely breathe . . . and having someone be really nice to you afterwards."

I tied her feet together, then anchored the ropes to the posts of the bed. Holding her legs open.

"Don't look. No . . ."

Once she was tied up like that, I buried my face between her legs. Dragging my tongue over her clitoris. Sticking to her like a parasite.

"I'm gonna go crazy, wait, stop, I'm coming. Wait, stop."

This is how I had my way with her. She was immobilized. Unable to move. Mine to have completely. The sight of a woman who can't move is enough to drive a man insane. I'd grab the rope and tighten up the bindings a bit more, until she started wheezing, then loosen them again and soothe her, pat her head, stroke her cheeks, before tightening the ropes and exercising my control. Her vagina squeezed my penis. The more I used the rope, the more sensitive she got, soaking my penis with her wetness. Beside myself, I drowned in her, and in the ropes. It felt like I had lived my whole life for this moment. If not for women, I would have killed myself before I made it very far in life.

"Ah, ahh, ahhhhhh!"

So I became a rope artist. Making a living as an employee at that tiny production company, I sometimes got to do kinbaku for the scenes and formed individual relationships with the women that I met that way. Spending whole days buried in the bodies of the women who would let me wrap their gorgeous bodies with my ropes. I might have seen nothing but women and rope, for the rest of my life. But gaining Kaminuma-sensei as a teacher vastly broadened my horizons. He gave my life a sense of meaning.

Sensei was the chief priest at a shrine. He knew a great deal about Shinto.

The Confessions of
Kazunari Yoshikawa: 2

"The shimenawa at a Shinto shrine are sometimes made from nylon or synthetic rope these days, but the real ones are made from hemp. Hemp rope, you see, creates a proper boundary . . . between this world and the spirit realm. Also protects people from evil."

"Makes a boundary . . ."

"The hemp is used to cordon off the sacred. In fact, cordoning it off this way is what makes it sacred in the first place. That's how the gods know it's okay to descend. Ropes also make a boundary between the gods and you and me, but I think this can be read two different ways. First being that the ropes purify a vulgar space and make it fit for divine habitation. The second being they protect the people from the gods . . . the will of the gods cannot be known; it is august, fearsome and mighty. Thus when mere mortals such as ourselves confront them, we must take pains to protect ourselves . . . Are you familiar with the legend of the Heavenly Cave, as told in the Kojiki and the Nihon Shoki? Amaterasu, goddess of the sun, went into hiding in a grotto made of stone, shrouding the world in darkness. In an attempt to lure her out, the gods that had gathered outside tried all kinds of things to capture her attention. Some gods even danced around in the buff. There was so much commotion that Amaterasu finally poked her head out to see what was the matter, whereupon they rousted her and pulled a rope that sealed the entrance of the cave, so that she couldn't go back in . . . This can be interpreted in many ways, but in my view, it signifies how rope can be used to seal off the entrance to a darkness that must not be entered, while asserting that not even gods can carelessly blow past a sacred barrier."

These talks with Kaminuma-sensei sometimes lasted deep into the night.

"So what makes hemp rope sacred? The Japanese have had a deep connection with rope since antiquity. In the Jomon period, which started in Japan around 13,000 BC, Japanese clothing was mostly made from hemp. I assume you know the etymology of Jomon: *rope markings*. The pottery designs made by pressing cord into wet clay gave this era its name. Like rope, clothing protects us from external forces. In a sense, it's another kind of demarcation, another barrier. Making these rope markings in the pottery goes beyond the aesthetic. By setting up a boundary, they fortify the spirit. But the main reason for all of this, I think, is that the hemp plant is the cannabis plant, you see."

". . . You mean the drug?"

"Cannabis contains two special chemicals, or cannabinoids, called THC and CBD. Larger stores of THC make the plant psychoactive. Most of the plants growing in Japan have lower stores of THC and much more CBD, which doesn't get you high. If you consider the influence of climate, Japan is not well-suited for the psychoactive strains. People like to point to this to explain why Japan hasn't historically used cannabis for its psychoactive effects, but they're actually mistaken . . . Archaeologists have found evidence that cannabis seeds were burned in ritualistic ceremonies in ancient Japan. Research and other evidence suggests that this was happening in third-century Yamatai-koku, when Priest-Queen Himiko ruled the land. Getting high on cannabis allowed not only the Japanese but people all over the ancient world to get closer to the gods. This made hemp sacred in and of itself. But in the Yamato Dynasty, led by His Majesty the Emperor, which came to power after the Yamatai-koku fell to ruin, the practice of using cannabis as a psychoactive substance all but disappeared."

Then what about using hemp rope to tie up women? Was that because women were sacred objects too?

"In case you weren't aware," said Kaminuma-sensei, speaking kindly, "but His Majesty the Emperor is the descendant of none other than Amaterasu, the chief deity of Japan. His Excellency is a descendant of the gods, and thus a god himself."

An image coalesced inside my head. His Majesty the Emperor was there before me, and strung around him was a taut cordon of rope. Hemp rope. Knowing I was unworthy of direct engagement with His Majesty, I had set the rope up as a barrier. And then I tied a woman up and cleansed her body, as an offering, His Excellency standing so high and mighty that I had to look straight up to see—

I shared these images with Kaminuma-sensei. But he got angry and beat me savagely.

"Blasphemy. His Majesty the Emperor is not a character for you to conjure in your mind. He has no need for the sort of woman you could proffer. Listen up, all right? If ever you do find yourself in the presence of His Majesty, get on your knees. No need for thinking or imagination. We're Japanese."

"Japanese . . ."

"We dwell in the land of the gods, one of the few holy places on this earth. And it's all here for His Majesty, don't you forget."

On my knees. Kneeling down, unconditionally, before Tenno Heika. His Majesty the Emperor. Inside of me, I felt my shame for having blasphemed melding with an effervescent joy. The miracle of how this lineage, descendants of the gods, had continued to this day. The sole nation on earth to be graced with such a ruler. Today the emperor has become something of a figurehead, much like the royalty in other countries, with politicians taking care of political matters, but I do not approve.

This period was something of a detour in the life of a man who lived for sex. It was a time when I was tantalized by dreams that would soon turn to dust. A brief spell of tranquility, arriving just before sex drove me crazy.

I started visiting my neighborhood shrine. The old me had never once considered the degree to which this thing called faith could give life meaning. Though one day at the shrine, somebody handed me a flier. "A NEW CONSTI-TUTION, FOR AND BY THE PEOPLE." Politics? Until that point, I hadn't known that the shrines also served, in part, as engines of constitutional reform. Making every effort to amend a constitution that had pledged to avoid war and aspired to an international peace.

What could I do in the service of His Majesty? Devote myself to politics? Though I was starting as a total out-sider, I did my best to learn. Right wing. Conservative. Unsure of where to pick up facts, I started off at some of the websites that cater to these inclinations. None of them inspired me enough to make me care. So I tried reading books, purchasing a bunch of titles. But I must have picked the wrong ones. None of them captured my interest.

The books were all bogged down by petty conflicts. Talking trash about China and Korea. Same old thing: yes to nuclear, yes to American military installations, peace clause of the constitution be damned, yes to an interventionist prime minister, screw the opposing party, screw the left, the liberal elite are a bunch of pansies. What did any of this mean? All I wanted, as a citizen of Japan, was to kneel before His Majesty the Emperor. All I cared about was his perspective. What were his thoughts on all of this? I would carry out his will. I could care less about these philistines and their opinions.

I had to meet His Excellency personally. On TV, he was nothing but an artificial image. I had to behold him with my own two eyes. I waited until New Year's, when the Imperial Palace opened to the public and His Majesty made his annual appearance, through a screen of glass, to greet the people of Japan.

I'll never forget the way I felt the first time I beheld His Majesty. Tenno Heika. My fervent awe gradually began to founder. His was the bearing of a mild-mannered personage. Gentle, and good-natured, he was an exponent of tenderness, an advocate for peace. What I pined for was a more tempestuous figure. Someone who would be our god and put the fear into our hearts. Could it be that I was just too dumb to understand his powers? I began to study the Kojiki and the Nihon Shoki. These two books enshrine His Majesty as a deity. During the war, the belief in imperial divinity was so absolute that research books were banned, their authors sent to jail. When I finished reading these two ancient texts, I experienced a mixture of disappointment and exhilaration.

What disappointed me was how not just His Majesty, but all members of the Imperial Family were regarded as descendants of the gods. Even though there could only be one direct descendant. And how the emperor in those days, despite being the supreme authority of the Shinto religion, was involved with Buddhism, of all things. Even though he was supposed to be a Shinto god. What the hell was that about? The facts that I found in those books were flavorless, much worse than anything I had imagined.

Don't get me started on the myths. Are we supposed to believe that the gods were born from puke and pee and poop? Or that the gods gave birth to the Japanese archipelago? How so? In that case, who made the other continents? Though it was I who was mistaken. The Kojiki and Nihon Shoki may be historical texts, but they are also mythical in nature and must be handled with the same discretion as one might bring to the Bible or the Quran. These myths take points of fact and convert them into tales even the masses, in our ignorance, can understand. All that matters is you take away the essential truths. Gods made the Japanese Islands. His Majesty the Emperor, Tenno Heika, is the descendant of Amaterasu, chief deity of Japan. Good enough. But I hesitate to add that

Amaterasu is depicted as a goddess. How could it be that Japan's chief deity is female? Could this be heresy? No, no way. The Nihon Shoki especially was long esteemed by the Imperial Court as a definitive history. But a goddess at the top? Then why doesn't Japan allow for matrilineal succession? I'm sure that this is but another sign of my confusion. Surely there must be a deeper meaning behind all of this, the sort of which a commoner like me could never fathom.

The parts I found exhilarating were the stories of Emperor Yuryaku and Emperor Buretsu. These were the tempestuous figures I had pined for. Emperor Buretsu, to keep himself amused, famously ordered for a group of women to take their clothes off and sit down on a bench to watch two horses copulate. Those who were not wet, upon inspection, were impressed into service, while those who had indeed gotten wet were put to death. The books actually say all that. Emperor Yuryaku was equally at ease with putting people to death, but he also demonstrated random acts of kindness to the populace. He was unpredictable, as a true god should be. In my view anyway.

Emperor Yuryaku or Emperor Buretsu could surely influence the weather without asking for assistance from some higher power. Their anger would summon gale-force winds, while in their better moods the skies would clear, and a refreshing breeze would blow. I thought about the lament of Yukio Mishima. Why, he asked, was it necessary for His Majesty the Emperor to declare himself to be a human being? What would Emperor Buretsu have done under the circumstances?

What if, for example, Emperor Buretsu was in power during the Pacific War? Under his furious command, surely the people would have fought until the last, until the country went up in a blaze of glory. The people would follow the emperor, at long last, up into the heavens. If Emperor Buretsu were alive today, we would fear his presence and surround his estate with a barrier of hemp. Emperor Buretsu would surely enjoy any woman that I offered him. The emperors of long ago had scores of concubines. I would put all the soul and skill that I could muster into tying up a woman and graciously offer her up to the emperor, and to the gods—

Watching me reeling, Kaminuma-sensei looked a little worried, but this time he smiled.

"As they say in Christianity, it's not a sin to doubt your faith. Reason being, it's only when we overcome our doubts that we arrive at our true faith, a faith that cannot be shaken. But here's a word to the wise. Faith and scholarship are mutually exclusive. If a time comes when you have to choose one or the other," said Kaminuma-sensei, looking deep into my eyes, "I want you to choose faith."

Rope artists will occasionally give private lessons. Private instruction for a wealthy client with an interest in kinbaku. One fateful day, when Kaminuma-sensei had become so horribly ill that it was like a thick gray cloud had landed on the surface of the earth, I taught one of his classes in his stead. To a man named Y. There are people in this world who you wind up wishing you had never met. But is that really true? Do I really wish that Y and I had never crossed paths?

When I stepped into the designated room, he was standing there, wearing a suit. No middle finger on his right hand.

Beside him was a naked woman. She introduced herself as Ami Ito.

The Confessions of Kazunari Yoshikawa: 3

"My lucky day. Sensei sends along a substitute."

Y had a deep voice. Probably in his fifties. A languid man whose movements and expressions betrayed little to no effort, but his facial features were unsettlingly sharp.

"I'm sorry for the inconvenience."

"It's fine, I know all about you."

Looking back, why did he know anything about me?

". . . I've been asked to work with you today on suspension variations."

This is exactly what it sounds like: suspending the woman from the ceiling. A form of rope torture, developed in the Edo period, when kinbaku got its start, as a way of tormenting or disciplining men and women alike. Attempted by an amateur without proper instruction, and a mishap is pretty much a guarantee. You need to study with a pro. There have been several cases where a woman strung up by an amateur suffered nerve damage or fell, with hazardous results.

"For starters, let's have a look at the basic suspension you've been practicing. If anything stands out, I'll let you know."

Y listened with a strange look on his face. When he realized it was him that I was talking to, he smiled. There were only three of us there in the room, including the woman. Who else could I have possibly been talking to?

Generally, the woman isn't fully naked during practice. Introducing your unclothed female partner to a rope artist is kind of a kinky thing to do. That's how I see it, anyway. For some reason, Ami Ito's skin was faintly sunburned in a pattern of horizontal bars. Y began to tie her up. At that point, she was just another beautiful woman to me.

"Ah . . ."

Ami's body floated up into the air. This binding was extremely complex. Y's ropework was superb; he didn't need a lesson. With her bound hands pulled over her head and anchored at her upper back, Ami was exposed up to her armpits. Floating in midair. Her legs were splayed, opening her vagina towards me. With an expression of intoxication, she parted her lips ever so slightly. I felt my breathing speeding up. With Ami thus disposed, Y grazed her nipple with a browsing finger. When she let out a little shriek, he gave her nipple a flick. And then another. And another.

"Oh, oh . . ."

With her suspended, Y touched his hand to her vagina. Ami shuddered and made a sound like she had been choked. She was having an orgasm. Almost instantly.

". . . Doesn't seem there's much that I could teach you."

"Hmm? Are you talking to me?"

The conversation had the strangest rhythm. I felt the blood speeding through my arteries. Y lowered Ami to the floor. Into a puddle of her wetness. She was shivering.

"Come on, I want to see you do it, sensei."

"But I'm . . ."

Ami's body had become acutely sensitive. In my years in the industry, I'd seen a number of women in this state.

"It's fine . . . Here."

Y passed me the rope. The inside of my mouth went dry.

Ami's gorgeous back twitched with the aftershocks of pleasure and the heightening excitement about what I was about to do to her. Her back had not been sunburned. The instant I had tied her wrists behind her, I knew she was the one. In fact, I knew as soon as I had brought her wrists together at her back. Her body answered me. I passed the rope two more times above her breasts and bound her stacked arms at the base of her spine. I had never met a body so responsive to the rope, or a woman so close to my ideal.

As if asking for permission, I found myself gazing up at Y, who was looking down at both of us. He gave me a friendly grin and nodded. I walked my lips over Ami's neck. Using a second rope, I constricted her breasts from above and below. Her upper body was tipping forward. If you lean forward like this, it hurts even more. A woman who could make herself come in a state of pain like this, hands tied behind her back and tipping forward, was beyond redemption. Kissing her neck from behind, I tickled Ami's nipples. She shivered as she squealed.

"Sensei, I understand you study Japanese mythology. Is that right?"

". . . I do."

"Do you know the story of Hiruko? First child of Izanami and Izanagi, the gods that gave birth to the Japanese islands. A poor kid who was cast off in a boat, just because he was disabled . . . That's the story of this woman. She's just like Hiruko. A high-profile mistress, thrown from the inner circle of Japanese politics. Another petty scandal."

"Hiruko . . ."

"But all over Japan, there are different legends about what happened to Hiruko after he was pushed into the waves. Japanese people are so kind. They came up with new stories where this poor little kid, set adrift by the gods, winds up finding happiness. The tragedy of one story is filled in by another . . . We need to write another story, to save this woman from the open seas. Don't you think?"

I put Ami on her back and kissed her ravenously, like a beast starved to the point of frailness.

". . . You can borrow my Hiruko, if you like."

"WHEN I'M TIED up, it makes me feel bereft of my humanity," Ami whispered to me. We were in a hotel, one specially equipped for BDSM guests. Just the two of us.

At the time, I was buried in debt. But thanks to a fake ID and a fake name that Y had given me, I was temporarily in the clear. I had gone from Takashi Yoshikawa to Kazunari Yoshikawa. Losing your first name feels like a departure from reality. Like you're a character in some kind of a story.

"Since I can't move, stripped of my free will . . . I don't have to do anything. Free will entails responsibility. But this is a release, from the responsibility to make your own decisions . . . The joy of being a slave. It's the only time I'm liberated from society, from existence, from my past and from myself."

I suspended Ami from a rope. A new self, Kazunari Yoshikawa. Using the reverse shrimp tie, a chest tie where both ankles are secured, and the body, slightly arched, is suspended from a knot in the middle of the back.

"Liberated from existence, I turn into a thing . . . It hurts being suspended. There's nothing I can do about the pain . . . but with you, I feel so reassured. The first time that you tied my arms behind my back, I was certain: *I know that I can trust him . . . He's the person I've been waiting for.*"

I remembered the way it felt, the first time I touched Ami, knowing that she, too, was the woman I was waiting for. This wasn't about love, but about getting what I'd wanted. Ami was saying the same thing. Though at the time, I didn't think much of it.

"As long as you're hurting me intentionally, I can feel safe. But once it stops being intentional, the safety vanishes."

I hoisted both her legs. Her body bent into a gorgeous, subtle curve.

"Ah, ahhhhhhh."

I tied a tenugui over her eyes. Robbed of vision, Ami floated in a sea of darkness.

"It hurts, it hurts . . . but I'll wait . . . for the moment, when it turns to pleasure, when I get, into the zone. At that point, when it happens, sometimes I can't, remember anything. Maybe it's like a runner, out for miles . . . past their limit, when they're hit, with runner's high. I guess some kind of, pleasure chemical, is released into the brain. Ah, ahhhh, I'll wait, until the hurt, the pain, turns into an erotic, pleasant feeling, agh, ahh, almost like in meditation . . . the pain, turns into pleasure, the torment, turns to love, the evil, turns to good . . . this is it, where everything, flips over . . . ah, ahh, I think . . . it's here."

I changed the tie around her legs, hoisting her even higher. This time with her legs wide open, to expose her vagina. It was a pose that Ami loved, because she was a nasty girl who craved humiliation. I pulled her up into the air. The ropes were tight. So tight.

"Ah, ahhhhhhh."

Her voice got louder, until she finally began to cry. I gagged her mouth with another tenugui, reducing the supply of oxygen to her brain to destroy her even more. She groaned through the tears. Coming apart. Ami.

"Mm, mmm."

If I pinched her nipples, it made her scream. Her body was shaking. I put my middle and ring fingers into her vagina. Caught in this crazed state, she came and came some more. I wondered if she'd made it. To the edge.

"Mm, ahh, mmmm."

A little more. Too much? Maybe just a little more. Deciding it was time, I loosened the ropes and laid her on the bed, then hastened to untangle all the ropes around her body. I had to hurry. My hands worked hastily. Ami was shaking. Crying. Once I had undone all the ropes, I held her in my arms.

"Are you okay?"

"Yeah, yeah."

"It's okay. That was scary, huh."

"Yeah."

"Really, everything's okay . . ."

I gave Ami a sweet kiss. Then I just held her. She cried and clung to me. On the inside, an erotic impulse, generated by the ropes, continued to provoke her. So sensitive that she could barely stand it, Ami slipped my penis into her and squeezed me hard. Not many men get to experience a woman so far gone she shows the whites of her eyes. Ami shook through multiple orgasms. But this time, she was under me. Her skin was marked all over by the gorgeous torment of the ropes.

"Oh, Ami, Ami."

Once more, I took the loosened ropes that had been set aside and wrapped them loosely around Ami. As she climaxed repeatedly in that mess of hemp, I clung to her and dragged my tongue over her body. I was entangled in the ropes, became a rope myself. It felt like we were separated from reality. Inside my mind, a staircase floated in the air. So tall I had to look straight up, a staircase made of stone, continuing forever. A figure dazzled from the steps. Someone looking down at us, from on high. The light was coming from their eyes, a light of tenderness, inside of which I felt my body melt away and disappear. Into that gorgeous, noble light, elevating me so far above the human, and instilling me with pleasure, the pleasure of the spirit realm . . .

"Ami . . . I want for us to give up everything we have . . . as an offering to the gods."

The Confessions of Kazunari Yoshikawa: 4

"Mm, mmahh."

Ami was tied up, this time by Y. In front of me.

"She's a pervy little lamb. Wouldn't you say?" asked Y. He was fingering Ami, who had been suspended so her legs were open wide. She cried and moaned. It didn't seem like she was fully there.

"Who do you like more, me or sensei?"

"Mmm . . ."

"Say it."

"Master Y . . . ah, ahhh, forgive me."

How was it that I watched them so attentively? Ami did not belong to me. Y had only let me borrow her. The heat of envy coiled around my throat and heart. My penis went erect.

". . . Hey, sensei, what do you think of this?"

Y tossed a photograph at my feet. A tree enclosed by a gorgeous fence of ropes slung between stakes. A number of paper ornaments were dangling from the ropes.

". . . It's terrific. Where is this shrine?"

"It's not a shrine. The photo may be black and white, but the streamers that you see are white and blue."

"Blue?"

"This was taken someplace in Northern Eurasia."

I was not sure what to make of this. A sacred zone like this, around a sacred tree, could only have been found at a Shinto shrine.

"Sensei, I know you're partial to Japanese things, to what you call originals . . . But do you really think the hemp ropes at Shinto shrines originated in Japan? As a matter of fact, the custom was brought over from Northern Eurasia."

"Huh?"

"Another thing, these Japanese myths . . . they aren't original to Japan either. They're a combination of tales brought over from the mainland, via the Korean Peninsula, or from places to the south, like Oceania."

". . . What are you saying?"

"And another thing, the sort of emperor you pine for. Tenno Heika. You realize that the word *tenno* comes from China? Just like all the Chinese characters . . . This isn't news. Any academic in Japan knows all this stuff. It's common knowledge in academia."

I was reeling. Well aware that Y was not the kind of person to spout lies about this sort of thing.

"Oh, did I make you sad? Huh? Sensei . . . sometimes when I see a woman dangling like this, it makes me want to roast her over a fire . . . but let's take her down for now."

Y lowered Ami to the carpet. Standing before her naked body, still tied up and breathing wildly, Y brought his fingers to his belt.

"I'm gonna fuck this stupid bitch, and I want you to watch."

The instant Y put his penis inside her, Ami let out a screaming sound, less of a moan than a snarl rising from the bottom of her gut. She trembled head to toe. Far more intensely than with me.

It felt as if my hands and feet had fallen off and run away. I was sweating profusely. I looked into it all after the fact, and what Y had told me was the truth, at least encyclopedically speaking.

The series of myths forming the basis of Japanese culture were derived by mixing together all manner of mythological traditions. On the Japanese islands, Eurasian myths of horsemen, which themselves absorbed the myths of Greece, blended with myths from Oceania and from the Korean Peninsula, so basically, from the entire Eurasian landmass. One would think these myths would then be propagated someplace else, but geographically speaking, Japan has no neighbor to the east but the Pacific Ocean. Hence why theorists speak of Japan as a "snow-drift culture." Everything blows east, where it gets mixed together and accumulates.

"I'm gonna strangle you. You like that?"

Same goes for the provenance of rope. In ancient

times, the cannabis plants used for making hemp rope were an invasive species. Brought over from the continent and cultivated in Japan. The practice of cordoning off sacred spaces using rope was an import from the shamans of Northern Eurasia. These shamans impersonated birds and did all sorts of ceremonial magic. The Inbe clan, a venerable family of antiquity said to have smoked cannabis, had ancestors who came over from the mainland and even had a patron deity modeled on a bird. Perhaps the word torii, spelled with characters for *bird* and *presence*, is in some way related. Though sadly, the Inbe clan fell from power as a result of a dispute with the Nakatomi clan, pushing them to the margins. Maybe this is why the practice of smoking cannabis disappeared from the imperial court.

"Isn't it obvious, though?" Y said to me, while he was having sex with Ami. "You really think the Japanese . . . popped out of the soil of these islands? The ancestors, of all the people, everybody living here today . . . came either from the mainland or the islands to the south . . . but then again, all human beings came from Africa . . . Strictly speaking, there's no such thing as an original."

Globalization. We talk about it like it's a recent phenomenon, but these exchanges have been happening periodically since antiquity. Japan has its traditions, a culture to protect. But these are the result of early instances of globalization, which hinged on the destruction and incorporation of other cultures. The things we call peculiar to Japan sit on a bottomless heap of history and culture arriving on these shores from overseas. And the same goes for the culture of other countries. It's common for the cultures of ethnic minorities to contain, upon examination, evidence of other cultures that that same minority group vanquished and assimilated in the past.

Tracing the origins of culture demands that we look back into myriad episodes of globalization, where one culture was baptized as another, bushwhacking through the dusky brush of history. I'm afraid that we could never make it all the way. To be proud of any aspect of a culture, we also need to be proud of the lineage of foreign influence that led to its creation.

"Do I hit that pussy good? Yeah?"

Y intentionally used crude and vulgar language. I recognize that when it comes to sex, this sort of language can be more exciting. Underneath Y's body, Ami groaned ecstatically. As if she had forgotten who or where she was.

"I'm gonna finish inside you, hm? Are you my little toilet bowl?"

"Yes. Yes."

"You're a nasty little toilet bowl, yeah, my little toilet, yeah."

Y came inside of Ami's gorgeous body. Like he was letting it all out. I had always used a contraceptive.

It became difficult to concentrate. I was utterly dazed.

But Y was in a daze himself, even more worn out than me, looking over at me like he was about to speak.

". . . Sometimes I wonder why I even bother finishing. Know what I mean?" Y asked me. As if he had forgotten that his sloppy penis was still hanging out. Startled as I was, I couldn't look away. His deflated body reminded me of a used condom on the ground.

"Nothing is more boring than the way the world looks right after you blow your load . . . Wouldn't you agree? A man's gotta recharge . . . Hahaha."

Then suddenly, Y gave me and Ami puzzled looks. Almost like he had lost track of why she and I were there. His eyes weren't landing anywhere specific. He looked like a used condom that had accidentally been animated, an object that, without a penis to define it, was irrelevant. His neck and back were shivering. I found him exceedingly disturbing.

"Should have roasted her over the flames after all . . . Oh, right."

Y took to his feet. Slowly, as if he had forgotten how to pull his pants up. He muttered something to himself and shook all over, after which he walked out of the room. As if me and Ami had not been there this whole time.

I moved closer to Ami, trying to rid the lingering image of Y from my mind. His presence was still clinging to her body.

". . . You okay?"

"I'm sorry . . . I'm sorry."

"It's fine . . . Let's take a shower."

"No way."

". . . Huh?"

"Master Y gave me his semen for a reason."

I literally could feel the blood go to my head. I almost fainted.

". . . You're crazy."

". . . It's gonna make it. At this rate, I'll get pregnant. If you want to stop it . . ."

"Huh?"

"You'll have to kill me first."

I had no idea what she was saying. But as she said it, for an instant, a smile crept across her face. A sharp spike had been driven through my heart. Was she being provocative? What was her problem? Before I knew it, I was handling the rope. What was I going to do? Kill her? Kill Ami? A puddle of volition in the corner of my brain wriggled like a vernal pool disturbed by flies. No, how could I possibly do such a thing? It was out of my hands; when I tried to drop the rope onto the floor, it wouldn't fall. It was caught between my fingers. The shape of the rope had changed, or seemed to. It was bending. Like it was trying to wrap itself around something. Around what?

The rope was in charge. Calling the shots. Like it was saying: hey, just do it, I'll show you what I want to do. I encircled Ami's body with the rope. This was not a tie in kinbaku. The rope enclosed her, like it was devouring her whole. The rope had crossed the boundaries of kinbaku. The rope was hungry. For a woman. For her life.

—If you wanted control, you should've tied me in a noose. It's out of your hands now.

"Mmmahhhhhhh."

Ami's shrieks snapped me out of it. She was collapsed on the floor, breathing wildly, the ropes slumped in a pile beside her. Bereft of the volition it had known but for a moment.

The Confessions of
Kazunari Yoshikawa: 5

I was alone, seated on my futon, playing with the ropes. At this point, I was living in a place that Y had rented for me. The room had a tatami floor. Tatami and rope have a lot in common.

Rough textures crept across my fingers and my palms. It can be dangerous for the fingers to become overly accustomed to an act. Sometimes you lose sight of the boundary between the fingers and the things they touch. Feeling that rough texture, in the moment I make contact, pulls me back into reality. This roughness is the boundary. But touching it creates curved lines—long, curving lines that lead to knots, which in turn generate more lines in which my fingers become tangled, making it hard to feel the roughness anymore. Rope has a spiraling shape. The spirals naturally give rise to curving lines that tie things up. I touched the rope for what could easily have been forever. Bringing my two eyes closer to the divots in the spiral of the braid, its twisted geometric shape. My lips entered the hollows.

Halfway through killing Ami, I could have sworn I heard the rope's voice. This should go without saying, but it's not like the rope was actually talking to me. It felt as if the expression of its spiraled shape had been converted, by my brain, into an annoyed human voice.

In Japan, we have the concept *yaoyorozu no kami*— kami are everywhere, inside of everything. It's common to bring things that have been in your possession for a long time to the shrine for proper disposal. By burning them in the sacred altar, you can release their spirit to the heavens.

Then what about the kami here? Inside the rope. A collective consciousness made manifest when all these countless strands of hemp twine come together. But alas, the "Japan" that I had thought was in this rope is slipping out of view. And why? Because in terms of spirituality and culture, Japan, like every country, is an amalgamation of all the other nations of the world. All cultures are constructed in the same way. Rope comes to us from Northern Eurasia. But some argue that rope itself originated in China, while others say the South of France. Who knows.

Enough with origins. Once this rope appeared before me, it became my deity. The kami of tradition, and Japan itself, became irrelevant to me. In my collection of ropes, four in particular are different from the rest. I could tell that they were different, no matter how I looked at them, or touched them, they just were. I knew that there was something there. The adult video production company that I'd worked for had gone out of business thanks to the explosion of illegally streamed videos. Ami had quit whatever she was doing for work. Once again, I was close to going broke.

Ami had told me something about Y. When was that? One time, she showed me a picture of a woman who looked just like her, but wasn't her.

"So yeah, as a matter of fact, I've had a little plastic surgery. And so has she."

Ami could turn into a chatterbox sometimes. Usually she was quiet, quick to find a corner for herself to hide away in, so for the most part, it was impossible to figure out what she was thinking, but on the rare occasion that the manic part of her manic-depressive personality took over, she got like this. Though I don't know, it's not like she went totally manic or something. In times like these, she sort of got a little confrontational, that's all.

"Y made us get it done, so we'd look more like his mother."

Targeting women that looked like his mother, Y made

them undergo plastic surgery, to enhance the similarity. He also made them change their makeup and their hair, their clothes, even their hobbies.

"But he isn't really into the whole mom thing . . . It's a front."

"A front?"

". . . It's all for show. When we first met, he realized that I looked like his mother and came up with this act. It's just an act. That's all it is . . . All men want from sex is someone like their mother, right? So they say. I guess he thought that he would try it out, to see if he would get a kick out of it. At first it seemed like it was working fine. That's why he found another girl with a similar vibe and made her get some work done too, though she didn't look as much like her as me . . . but he got sick of it. Imagine changing someone else's face, then losing interest . . . Sometimes he tells me that I'm tied up even when there's nothing tied around me. He calls it an invisible knot and laughs like he's annoyed at me. Says that in a certain sense, that makes me like his mother too . . . I'm not sure what he means by that, though."

". . . What's his deal?"

"I'm not sure. He says he's an investor, but he's probably a yakuza. Or maybe in some kind of shady business. Or unemployed. Who knows. I've heard he has some kind of connection with the US Army . . . but I'm not sure."

Y had talked about a petty scandal. Until a few years

back, Ami had been romantically involved with a certain politician. An incompetent second-generation Diet
member who had inherited his father's constituency and
belonged to a sizeable faction. He broke her body and her
spirit and tossed her aside like a piece of trash.

As soon as a reporter from one of the weeklies had
caught wind of their affair, he was transferred to a new
post. His editor was fired. Ami was not about to talk,
but the politician felt no remorse. I guess he had it out
for Ami. That's when he passed her off to Y. He said he
wanted Y to fuck her up for pissing him off. On the night
when he showed up with Ami, though, Y shot the politician with a pistol. Right there in the hotel. Like he was
swatting absentmindedly at a mosquito.

"I was shocked. What I had done, I mean, was pretty
normal . . . right? But things stopped being normal really
quick. I didn't care what happened anymore, so when I
was handed off to Y, it barely registered. I'm not sure if
this is going to make sense to you, but if a person is stuck
in a particular situation long enough, their emotions sort
of dry up . . . Still, though, when I saw the blood spraying
from that politician's body, the most gorgeous red that I
had ever seen . . . for a second, it was like my heart had
been resuscitated. I felt it beating in my chest."

That's right. Ami said this with a smile. The closer that
my memories get to the present, the blurrier they are. Even
as I write this, I'm not certain I can trust my thoughts.

"Y is incredible, though . . . Once he had me in that dark place, hardly enough light to see, it felt like I had disappeared. Like I had vanished in a puff, just like that . . . into a place that you could never ever reach."

Ami was smiling again. I pushed her down and pulled her clothes off, blue underwear and all. My fingers, strangely long and thin, turned into spirals that encircled her. I surrendered to the rope. That it might take me places I could never go myself. These ropes, these lines, were beckoning to me.

"Ah, ahhhhh."

Ami's body was suspended. It was a messy, careless tie, but not without its calculations. Beautiful. At least to me. Not something that a human being could make. Tied in a figure eight, the loose end of the rope dangled in the air. Telling me its work was not yet done. I grabbed the end of the rope. I could see it. It was like I under-stood what to do next. I wrapped the rope around her. Ami cried out. Good. Let's hear some more of that, the voice of life being extinguished. The ropes looked happy. The sound of her voice made the ropes bob and sway. I felt a sense of stillness. Just as I thought something was off, Ami leaned forward, so that her neck took all the weight. She was doing it on purpose, as a sign of her devotion, in order to choke herself in the entanglement of rope. I rushed to lift her neck and freed the ropes to let her down onto the floor. What the hell, I think I said to her. But she just glared at me. You coward. That's what she called me

Looking back, I realize that at that point, Ami was no longer Ami anymore. And maybe she had been like that already when I met her. I couldn't help but feel as if for years, Ami had been giving up, slowly but surely, her actual personality, a part of her that I could never know. I had the suspicion that the Ami there before me was an altogether different person from whoever she had been, what, ten years earlier. But in that case, who was she now? Whatever person she had been before all of this happened was dying a slow death inside her brain, where something else was taking over. It was moving through the throes of pleasure toward a spontaneous death, like a reverberating sound, existing only insofar as it was moving. She had lost her individuality, to the point where it was hard to say if anything that she was doing she was doing on her own. Like she was just a humming in the ears, a life that was already over.

Out of money, I filmed myself and Ami going at it and tried to sell the video to adult video companies. But they said they were "confused." That the scene where I went after her with the vibrator was okay, but the stuff with the kinbaku was "confusing."

What exactly did they find confusing? The fantastic angles of the tie I used to cross the ropes over her torso, so that they dug into the skin under her breasts and pulled them up and to the right? The subtle way in which the ropes extending from her shoulders down her back had been positioned just a tad bit further to the left than usual?

Or had it been this ideology, unconcerned with what the joints and muscles could withstand, in which the body existed solely for the pleasures of the rope? Or the double-take in which the body's delicate equilibrium was made to look like it was actually quite sturdy, but only as a way of proving just how delicate it was? Or the disjointed sanctity created when a solitary rope, encompassing the thigh, is intercepted by another rope from above?

". . . They're calling me," Ami sometimes said.

". . . Who is?"

". . . Not who. It's not a person. They're calling for me. Waiting for me."

Ami was hanging there, before my eyes. The rope was out of my hands. An aching in my body and the raggedness of my breath convinced me it was me who had suspended her. But I wasn't alone. Standing beside me were Y and, oddly enough, Kaminuma-sensei. I was so shocked to see them that I gulped. Ami's body was suspended in the shape of the sacred manji, each limb bent at a right angle, perpendicular to the next.

The way Ami was tied up, the ropes would choke her more with every movement. Had I done this myself?

When? Ami's beautiful body was being twisted, choked, and ripped to shreds. I thought it was so beautiful. Never had I seen kinbaku look so beautiful before.

It was hard to tell if Ami was in a state of rapture, or writhing in pain, or climaxing continuously out of pleasure. Her struggle cinched the rope around her neck. My body stiffened. As if it were held captive by an awful certainty that I must not step out of line, for I was in the presence of the sacred. My penis was getting harder by the second.

—*Good. Good. Finally.*

". . . She was on the verge of killing herself anyway," said Kaminuma-sensei, talking over the voice of the rope, though terror drained the color of his face.

—*Good. This is it.*

"Might as well have people watching, instead of dying all alone at home."

Ami's body convulsed violently. I really should have stopped things then and there. But my body had become one with the ropes around her body. As if I had become part of their spiraling form, I felt myself twisting around Ami, squeezing the life out of her. That life proved much more stubborn than expected. This was how it had to be. I rode the wave. Feeling myself channeling the ropes, from a distance, I choked her even harder. It was like a voice was yelling at me to get on with it and end her life. To finish off this life left dangling by a pesky thread. I gave it everything I had. Crushing her life, with mine. A little further. Just a little further, and this life would be over. But how much? How much further could she go? Her convulsions traveled down the ropes, to their excitement, shaking my body. Harder. More. The ropes went lax; I was certain I had killed her, but when I doubled down and closed the ropes even more tightly, squeezing out the last dregs of a life that had exploded through its death and into softness, I experienced a convulsion of my own, as if I had contacted her very essence. I flailed around as I ejaculated. In my pants. Together with the violent surge of pleasure, I had seen a flickering black and white image playing at the back of my mind, I was convinced, of a slippery round object being crushed. My legs went numb, and the tears streamed down my face. What was I . . . ? Ami had stopped moving.

". . . All right, all right. Not as good as I'd expected, though."

I was on my knees. Kaminuma-sensei and Y lowered Ami's body to the floor. The camera was running.

"Hey, Y?"

". . . Hm? You talking to me?"

"Did you know that this would happen, when you said that me and Ami could . . ."

Y gave me a dubious look. But eventually, he let his gaze fall to his finger. When they were letting Ami down, it seemed that he had twisted it. What happened to his finger was his own fault, of course, but he looked at me like I had gotten in his way and was to blame.

"I thought it would be funny if it did."

RIGHT OUTSIDE OF the apartment Y had rented for me, they put up a new apartment building that made me feel so claustrophobic I could hardly breathe. And if I looked out of the back window as the sun went down, all that I could see were the silhouettes of three crosses. They were telephone poles, mind you, but three crooked crosses was all that I could see. The image of Christ, nailed to the cross and dying for the sins of humankind, is continually explored by painters and sculptors, who pin him to the cross for all eternity, as an expression of worship. In the past, people would flagellate themselves to taste his pain. If they felt pleasure in the process, was it coming from a holy place, or from an immense blasphemy? Christ was crucified upon the cross. If this wooden object, the thing to which they nailed, and in so doing, killed him can be viewed in a holy light, then the four ropes that killed Ami must be holy too. Though sadly, I was unable to gain purchase on this way of thinking. The crosses, and their solitary god, only left me feeling punished. If the Christian god is all-seeing, he had not overlooked me in Japan. I would ask the gods of my homeland for help, but Shinto has no teachings in which murderers are saved.

His Majesty the Emperor—I was no longer worthy of his graces. And god, the Christian god, was not a force that I could turn to in distress. The Christian god was unfamiliar to me. To cast myself as a believer would be foolish. Before me were the four ropes that had been behind the death of Ami. Even if they contained sacred spirits, I lacked the mental fortitude to count on them for anything.

—Then maybe you should die yourself? If you're too scared to follow me. You've served your purpose.

If Ami was like Hiruko, abandoned by Japan, I had carried out a national directive. But I had gone astray from the kami of Japan. As a gesture of solidarity with Hiruko, my Hiruko, I decided I would undertake the customs of antiquity that had been banned by the Imperial Court. Funerary customs of the past, in which a family marked the passing of a close relation by cutting their hair short and drawing blades across their thighs. A carryover from Northern Eurasia, these customs had been outlawed long ago by the highest authorities. But I would go against the ban.

I cut my hair off with a kitchen knife and used the blade to cut my thighs. The horrific pain reorganized my mind. Of course. By murdering Hiruko, had I not carried out the will of the gods? But no, I wanted none of that. Lost in a maze that had no rhyme or reason, I was suspended in midair, an offense and nothing more, no hint of salvation or warmth. What about Emperor Buretsu? . . .

The ban on cutting hair and self-harm had been enacted well after his time, during the reign of Emperor Kotoku. And what about the Inbe Clan, fallen out of favor with the court? No, none of this felt right.

Losing my mind, I took the woman that Kaminuma-sensei asked me to break in and tied her up, like I was kidnapping her. If I had had my way, I would have made an offering of her to Ami, may she rest in peace, and to the gods, though I had lost my faith. The woman was blindfolded, so I couldn't see her face, but somehow she reminded me of Ami. The god inside of me was dead. I had to make another offering. I spent all of my days in mourning clothes. Call me crazy. Maybe I was.

"Poor thing," a voice said. When does this fit in?

I looked up, and standing there, beside Y, was a gorgeous woman.

The voice was hers.

She said her name was Maiko Kirita.

The Confessions of
Kazunari Yoshikawa: Conclusion

Y disappeared, leaving the two of us alone. She brought me to the apartment where Ami Ito used to live, when she was still alive. Ami had never brought me there. It was like visiting the room of a college boy. It was possible that

Y had set her up there out of some kind of a fondness for the past. It wasn't until we had reached the entrance that I noticed Master Maiko had been wearing not high heels but an unlikely pair of sneakers. She told me, a bit embarrassed, that she liked to go for walks.

"So you're good with ropes, huh?" Master Maiko asked me. She sounded deeply curious. Staring at me, she stripped down to her purple camisole. "Show me."

I took the four ropes that had murdered Ami from my bag. When I held them to Master Maiko's pale skin, I shuddered. Knowing I was crossing a line. At this point, I can see this was anxiety. I did my best to gather myself, unsettled as I was about the trembling of my fingers, and managed to tie Master Maiko's hands behind her back. But something didn't feel right. The ropes were sluggish, almost like they were resisting. I felt alienated by the hemp.

"Oh, that's nice," Master Maiko told me. But I was unable to see the motion of the ropes. I was unsure of what I was supposed to do. I remembered my experience and training. What to do next if it felt nice. As I tied her up, Master Maiko made a sound like she was sighing. It was too beautiful for words. I say that, but my penis wasn't hard. Still, I had to make this satisfying. Using the third rope, I restrained both her legs.

"Mmm, that's nice. Ah, ah, hahaha!"

Master Maiko was laughing. Like she couldn't hold it

in. My blood went cold, as my limbs turned to jelly. She gave me an apologetic look.

". . . I'm so sorry. I didn't mean to laugh."

She brought her face to mine. That absurdly gorgeous face.

". . . I'll make it up to you," she said. "How about I make your dreams come true?"

Master Maiko undid the ropes herself. My knots are not as tight as some. She grabbed the black necktie I was wearing, in my mourning, and gently pulled me down. Soon I was on my knees. But Master Maiko squatted too, and pulled on my tie even harder, so that I was prone to the floor. She stepped on the tie and stood up in one motion. I remained on my stomach, unable to get up. All I could do was regard Master Maiko from the floor.

That's when Master Maiko restrained me.

Since I'm a rope artist, I'd obviously been tied up before. It's important to have someone tie you up, so that you know the way it feels. Though I had only ever done this with Kaminuma-sensei.

The instant that I felt the hemp rope bind my arms behind my back, I started to cry. For having murdered Ami. For having lost touch with the gods. For the vacuum that was my life. For the fact I had no idea what to do next. For the fact that I had no real talent as a rope artist. Ami had just wanted somebody to kill her. It takes courage to die, but if you're going to be killed, it may as well come at a moment of ecstasy. A rope maniac like me was the ideal person for the job.

". . . You poor thing," Master Maiko said to me, pulling the ropes tighter. "You've wanted somebody to do this to you for so long, haven't you?"

I'll have you know my penis was quite hard by now. But she was wrong. No, not for so long at all. Just since I murdered Ami.

"Wow . . . look at you. All worked up. Ought to be ashamed of yourself."

Though I didn't know this until later, Master Maiko was basically a sub, but at random she could flip into a dom. Plenty of people enjoy both, of course. In this line of work, we call them switches.

I was sitting on my heels, hands tied behind my back. Master Maiko took the opportunity to stomp my penis. Miserably erect as it was.

"I'll go ahead and crush this for you. That would solve everything, right?"

I felt my throat close up, as my body trembled with fear. The pain of being stepped on transformed into pleasure. I looked up at Master Maiko, pleadingly. Surrendering my agency. Letting her decide what would become of me. Setting the baseline for good and evil. My life was in her hands. The tears kept coming. It was getting harder to breathe. I had been stripped of selfhood.

"Don't even think of coming yet."

". . . I can't help it."

The second that I spoke, Master Maiko kicked my penis. In the midst of the excruciating pain, I ejaculated. I had never come like this before. My shoulders and my back muscles were trembling. But the humiliation set me free. Master Maiko owned me, through and through. In my humiliation, I could resign myself to being who I was. Surrendering my very consciousness to her.

". . . Poor thing."

Master Maiko held my head to her breast. I was so thankful. The tears gushed forth once more. To think that she would let a scumbag like me bury his face in her pillowy breasts. She may have called me a "poor thing," but Master Maiko tied me up again, tight as ever. "Poor thing. Poor thing." The pain was so intense I screamed. Master Maiko was crying, too, like she was taking pity on me. Even though she was the one who'd tied me up. After that, I can't remember anything. From what I hear, I ejaculated two more times.

From then on, I spent almost all my time restrained, either at this apartment or my own. My place, because of the tatami, was more appropriate for kinbaku. I was free. In the sense of being powerless. Free from my life, from my misdeeds, and from my worries. As her slave, I no longer had to make any decisions. Her will and hers alone dictated my existence. But I retained the pleasures of excruciating punishment. Like somebody who had a pet incapable of moving on its own, Master Maiko worked around me, cleaning up the place, in her own messy way. Sometimes I would masturbate in front of her and Y. They never laughed, just watched me like I was the most miserable thing. Seeing my semen shoot across the floor made me feel so humiliated that my blood cooked in my skin. If Master Maiko was feeling horny, she would let me lick her vagina, sitting on my face so I could give her cunnilingus. I was no more than a human vibrator to her. As she showered me with piss or walked across my face, I thought about how I had tried to take an interest in politics, so long ago. This, I told myself, was an ideal model for the nation state. Meekly surrendering all choice to those in power, without any opposition. That was pleasure. "Poor thing." Master Maiko hugged my dirty face. Cradling me. I was unfortunate and fortunate at once.

Master Maiko could adapt her personality to different people. At the core she was as kind a person as they come, though sort of naive, but when she got it in her head to make somebody happy, her excessive kindness naturally drew out the other person's innermost desires. Even if that same desire left them dead. Though I wouldn't call her deranged, she was oddly naive when it came to the question of other people's mortality. If her kindness destroyed the other person, she still felt bad for them.

What kind of person was she anyway?

I have no idea how Master Maiko and Y met. But one

time Master Maiko hinted at their story. She said that Y had a dark chasm inside of him, that she felt really bad for him, but that lately he'd been acting strange. That lately he had more glitches than ever. And that he said it was her fault and blamed it all on her.

WHAT DID IT mean to tie a person up with something as sacred as hemp rope? I don't think it was actually about offering a woman's body to the gods, like I used to believe. No, it was a way of overcoming the mundaneness of the world and our insipid daily lives. In the Edo period, when kinbaku was created, the peculiar sense of beauty people experienced upon seeing a criminal tied up consisted of not only sexual desire, triggered by the sight of human bondage, but of an envy towards a person who had acted out, beyond the law. But it also held the promise of transcendence, since becoming entangled in the sacred meant being transported to an entirely different world. In that sense, kinbaku performed using hemp rope is about crossing over barriers of every kind. Once we have left behind the world we know, we can do anything at all. This can lead to happiness of a supreme variety, but if you make the sort of mistakes that I made, you may well find yourself in dangerous terrain and meet your ruin.

I pleaded with Master Maiko not to use hemp rope to tie me up. Saying that I wasn't worthy of the hemp.

I feel like I'm about to forget everything, but as long as I remember who I am, I'll do my best to leave a record of the sort of person that I used to be. Before Y and Master Maiko swallowed me up. Though looking back, it makes a lot of sense that they would swallow someone with an ego as trifling as mine.

As Master Maiko tied me up, I thought about my new name, Kazunari. The name that Y had chosen for me, reclined in front of me. In my analysis, the name has connotations of taking care of business, one big task after another. Though in my case, only one matter of business had been settled. My whole life had been worthless, except for murdering Ami. The end. From what I can recall, I sort of chuckled when Y told me that my new name would be Kazunari. It takes a special kind of wickedness to pack a joke about a person's fate into a fake identity—

AMI. I'LL BE coming for you soon. Just because I've made it this far doesn't mean I'm off the hook. My life is over. I really should have tried to save you. I wish I could have helped you, the real you, before that politician got to you, the version of you lying torpid in the deepest reaches of your consciousness. We could have started over. That would have been right. Imagine how much fun we could have had, with a different kind of kinbaku. A lot more fun. As we grew old together . . .

But it's too late for that . . . This life of mine, what was it all about? Had I been called by the ropes, a feeble man like me, only to accomplish that one task? Nothing but tragedy and destruction to look forward to. What led me here? Was it the doing of the gods? No, I tend to think the gods were not to blame. Of course I'll accept full responsibility, but I think that there's a kind of flow, or energy, that leads us . . .

. . . Though honestly, what is life about?

9

"If you're going to penalize me, let's get it over with," said the chief priest, Kaminuma. But at the shrine, he went by Ishida. He had welcomed us as guests into his house, which was stuffy and old-fashioned, but every inch of it was polished to a fussy sheen.

"After watching Yoshikawa take Ami Ito's life, I started having nightmares. Her limbs strung up like that . . . into a manji. No death could take a more beautiful or more miserable shape. It was a murder, any way you looked at it, though for some reason it was classified as a suicide by hanging. I became afraid of Y, and of his background."

From a distance, we could hear the voice of a young girl.

"I told him that I wanted out, that I was going to turn myself in. But then he sends this woman over for me. I'm thinking, a woman, for me? When a man reaches a certain age . . . But this woman, she has a little kid with her. A girl. Got pregnant working at a soapland, so she doesn't know who the dad is . . . I felt sorry for them, so I took them in, and they're living with me to this day. I'm an old man, you see. Instead of hush money, Y gave me the gift of a loving family to support . . . I've never met a man who hates life as much as him. He knew that I would suffer, caught between the pressures of this loving family and atonement for my sins . . . Must have figured, too, that I'd set aside a modest inheritance for them and eventually kill myself . . . This shrine claims to bless its visitors with happy marriages . . . Dark humor if you ask me."

The chief priest glared at me. Unable to make eye contact with Yamamoto, on account of her resemblance to Ami Ito.

". . . Where's Y these days?" I asked.

"No idea . . . Come to think of it, I never learned his actual name. I'm being serious. I understand that Yoshikawa did some sleuthing and figured it out, but Y must have still had a great deal of control over his thoughts, since he was too scared to write down anything but his initial."

He didn't look like he was lying. No reason to cover for him now.

"Take this thing," the priest said, handing me the notebook. Through the sounds of the girl's lilting voice, off in the distance, his own voice trembled. "Do whatever you want with it."

SLUMPED DOWN IN the passenger's seat, Yamamoto fixed her eyes on the upper portion of the windshield. Nothing but dull clouds to see.

"Yesterday, you said you have a hard time with wide-open spaces . . . Is that a carryover from, you know, the way they trained you?"

"I'm not sure if they did it on purpose . . . but I guess it makes sense. He kept me in a really tight space."

"Like a cage?"

"Cage? Yeah, basically. He threw my food at me and told me I looked right at home . . . Why do you ask?"

". . . Simple. I've heard enough to have a pretty good idea of who Y is."

I stepped on the gas. The rundown shrine slipped away, into the distance.

"When you asked if I could save you, did you mean from dying?"

Yamamoto didn't answer me. She just stared through the windshield. Looking up.

"If I wind up arresting Y, he's going to try to kill you. Once he's deprived of his freedom and tuckered out, he'll hire somebody to do the job. For the fun of it . . . I know you know this, but a man like him is never going to change. We could try giving you a bodyguard, but if he sticks it out and hunts you down, year after year, it'll be hard to fend the goons off. Besides, I'm guessing Y's controlling more than just your head. Probably your wallet too."

". . . Yeah. My debt."

"How much we talking?"

"I couldn't say. It's not the sort of thing where I could file bankruptcy and make it disappear. These weren't your average loans."

Yamamoto watched the sky, up and away.

"I'll say this much," I said. Realizing my voice sounded a little cold. "I think we can rule out the existence of any kind of god."

10

I used the spare key to open the door.

An orange light was glowing at the back of the apartment. At moments going dim, like it was about to go out.

I took off my shoes and walked across the fluffy carpet, down the hall. In the middle room, a man was sitting on a leather sofa. Not looking at me.

". . . Unbelievable. I never thought you'd find me."

He had no middle finger on his right hand. A suitcase open in the corner. Empty.

". . . Someone must have talked. Though I could have sworn basically nobody knew my real name."

The orange light flickered off, then came back on, a little brighter. The air in the room was extremely dry. My eyes were itchy. I blinked on purpose.

"I found the notebook Yoshikawa left behind," I said. My voice was hoarse. "Buried at the shrine where Kaminuma works. You know, your old kinbaku teacher . . . One might say that Yoshikawa left this memoir as an offering, almost like a haniwa."

". . . And?"

"The notebook says it all. Though it took all of my attention to assemble all the pieces . . . You found two women who reminded you of your mother and made them both get plastic surgery. Both of them have a peculiar tendency to tuck themselves away in narrow spaces. The notebook says that at the time when Ami Ito met Yoshikawa, she had these horizontal bars sunburned into her body. Since she evidently didn't have them on her back, it stands to reason that you had her lying face up, in a cage by the window . . . From all the different possibilities, it makes the most sense that the two of them would feel relaxed in tiny spaces because you conditioned them to feel that way. Yamamoto confirmed that you had her locked up in a cage for sure. But you also made a point of telling both these women in their cages, dressed up like your mother, that they looked like *they were right at home*. You made up this idea of the invisible knot, saying they were tied up even when there weren't any ropes around them. And you said that in a way, this made them even more like your mother . . . I came to the conclusion that your mother was incarcerated . . . And another thing. I took a closer look at Maiko Kirita's calling card and found skin oils in just two places, on the left edge and the right edge, like it had been pinched on the sides. At first I thought that maybe

Kirita had handed it to Yoshikawa with one hand, and Yoshikawa had accepted it with one hand too, but I was wrong. Yoshikawa was her slave, so if his master, Kirita, had handed him a card, he would have taken it with both hands, on his knees, leaving skin oil all over both surfaces. Someone else planted the card there. And by someone I mean you. You touched it once when you pulled it out of Kirita's card case. Then touched it again when you slipped it into the planner . . . Because you're missing your middle finger, you have to pinch it on the edges, hence where you left the oils. There's only one reason you would put Kirita's card in there. To frame her and put her behind bars. I take it you were a little scared of her, but you were unable to stomach the idea of someone taking her away, so you wanted to keep a handle on her, even if you were apart . . . This made me wonder whether you may have put your own mother in jail for the same reason. People have a way of doing the same thing over and over. Especially as they approach the end."

". . . Hah."

"We sent digital photographs of Ito and Yamamoto to all of the women's prisons in Japan, looking for a close match. One woman came up, though she looks less like them than I expected. She killed her husband, and despite a lack of evidence, they sentenced her because of her son's testimony. Following her release, she made no attempt to reconnect with her son before throwing herself into a pond . . . Though it wasn't the same pond where Togashi died, it was a very similar pond, all things considered. I knew this wasn't a coincidence. All I had to do was look up the son's name . . . I tend to think you took a special interest in Togashi because you and him had a few things in common? You were both desperate. Everything about the case says as much. At first, you thought that you could put the guilt on Kirita. You thought it might be fun to leave the body where it was, upping the ante, so that Kirita would get locked up, just like what happened to your mother. All over again. Since you seem to know a fair amount about fake IDs, you could disappear abroad if Kirita told them about you. But right away, you regretted putting it on Kirita, so you tried to pass the blame to someone else. Which I suppose is how the manager of the escort agency that Mari Yamamoto used to work for, who nobody can seem to reach, wound up brutally murdered. Nice flourish, with that little suicide note, by the way. But then Togashi showed up. You seemed to like this part a lot. Using Kirita, you passed along that planner, where you left clues that led to Mari Yamamoto and the apartment where you staged the body of the manager. I showed Yamamoto a sample of Togashi's handwriting, but she said the writing in the planner couldn't have been his. The script was messier, she said, like it was written by a kid. I know you wrote it, though you didn't seem to care that it was barely legible, because of your missing finger. After going back and forth about whether to frame Mari Yamamoto or her manager, you settled on Yamamoto, which meant his body was no longer necessary, so you had one of your grunts take it away. If Togashi had been able to kill Yamamoto, this thing would all be over. But he couldn't bring himself to do it."

I brought my hand to my belt.

"You killed Togashi," I said. "Didn't you."

"That's right. I've never seen you before, but I saw him twice."

Y pointed a pistol at me. But I had beat him to it, drawing a split-second earlier.

". . . You're a detective. I thought only officers on patrol were allowed to carry guns."

Y rearranged his face into a sort of smile.

"Wow, haha . . . Never in my life would I have dreamt of winding up in a standoff like this."

He could no longer look away. Y opened his mouth again. That crooked mouth of his.

". . . I did it all. Literally everything, for my entire life . . . and now," he said, leaning back into the sofa, "look what's happened."

That wasted body. Sharp as his features were, the muscles of his face were sagging. His eyes were on the prayer beads at my wrist.

"Reality has started looking like a video to me . . . I've *lost interest*. If there's a person there in front of me, they don't feel like a person. Just another image. A picture you can touch. I've forgotten the majority of my past. I may as well have you fill in the blanks. You could tell me that I was abused, or deprived of love by both my parents, go nuts. One day, I woke up and it was like this . . . When I found that Kirita girl, I got excited for the first time in a long time. But it was no good. That woman is dangerous. It's strange, I can't tell if I lured her in, or if she lured me . . . Poor thing, she used to say to me. Said she wanted to make my dreams come true, anything I wanted . . . Like Yoshikawa used to say, that woman had a way of drawing out a person's innermost desires, except that there was nothing that I hadn't done that I wanted to do. So I started getting real weird, thinking up new things to do. Figured, may as well. Does that make me desperate? I can see why you might think as much. Everything there is to know about this case, all of the twists and turns, are a reflection of the fluctuations of my mind. And now you've followed all those winding lines back to the source."

Blister packs of pills had been torn open on the coffee table. Xanax and Etizolam. They looked like candy.

"Yuichi Hayama," he said. "I know all about you."

Y gave me another of his little smiles. He had lowered the gun slightly, but now he pointed it at me again.

"You're a detective at Ninagawa Station, but you used to be on the first division . . . In Japan, it's a rare event for a detective to kill somebody. But you seem to have stumbled into *that kind of a situation* several times. Born under a bad sign. Not for me to say whether you brought it upon yourself, or if this was the life that you were born to live. By chance, you found yourself in the middle of a battle between rival gangs and killed two people, without actually firing a gun yourself. The average citizen is oblivious to how many people get away with murder, without the cops lifting a finger. I've shown up with my gun at the homes of several of these people, who had thought they got away, and shot them dead . . . though every time, it was to help somebody in need. I've forced a few people to commit suicide too, to pay for what they did with their own lives. The people close to you seem to be dying all the time . . . lovers included."

I made an effort not to alter my expression. I steadied my breath, making sure he didn't notice. Most people hold their breath before they shoot. They do it unconsciously, because their muscles will go soft if they exhale. I tried to gauge Y's breathing, but I couldn't figure it out. For all I knew he was going to shoot me on an outbreath.

". . . You're not a normal guy. Am I lying? I can't believe you turned Maiko down. It would have been a real fun game if you had fallen hard for her. You would have done your best, relying on your moral fiber or what have you, manipulating her the way you do with everyone else, but things would go south quick, because of me, and she'd destroy you . . . Wait."

The life drained from his face even more.

"Hey . . . there's one thing that I couldn't figure out. I'd actually known your colleague Togashi for a while. The second I saw him from across the room, at this club I run, kind of as a hobby, I knew he wasn't normal, and that made me real excited . . . I thought I might get Maiko to seduce him, then destroy him, just for fun. Maiko, nice person that she is, accepts the darkest parts of me, and she proved it by seducing him, but then push came to shove, and she started feeling sorry for him, so things didn't go so well . . . When I told Maiko to go after you, though, there was something oddly cool about the way she said okay . . . Is it possible she thought that you would get the better of me? Could she have been trying to kill me, out of kindness? Hey . . . if you had to pick a way to go."

"You prick," I said. My throat was parched. "If you can get away from me, what's next?"

"What's next? Are you asking me?"

He must have been caught off-guard, in the middle of a thought. He drew a blank; even his eyes were vacant.

"I'm done with life. And I'm bringing everything down with me. Lately, I've found myself regretting things the day after I do them. It just sort of pops into your head, know what I mean? Maybe I'll kill Mari Yamamoto, or maybe I'll kill Maiko, or maybe I'll find someone else to kill. If I wind up in prison, it'll only kick this pattern into overdrive. I'll give my lawyer the instructions in secret code when he comes by to see me. And when I hear the news from out-side, about how much of a mess I've caused, the corners of my mouth will go up, what, a fraction of an inch . . . So you see?"

Y gave me a long, hard look. Staring deep into my eyes. With eyes too weak to strain.

"You have no choice but to shoot me. And the second that you do, I'll shoot you back. Who survives will be decided by where we're hit and the placement of our arteries and organs."

Mine was already cocked. Move a finger, and the gun would fire.

"If you're lucky enough someone comes to save you, and you live to see another day, as the detective who killed me, my associates are going to come after you. So no matter what you do, you're dead . . . What? You don't seem scared. I noticed your throat was dry. Was that because of the air in here? What is it, huh? You want to die?"

". . . No."

"Then what is it? Are you giving me a pass?"

"No."

". . . What's your deal? Don't tell me that you care what's going to happen to the others."

The others. I didn't know Maiko Kirita or Mari Yama-moto very well. Certainly not well enough to risk my life trying to save them. Then what was this about? I couldn't bring myself to leave the two of them behind.

But I knew this wasn't righteousness or kindness. What was it?

"*I guess you and I are soulmates,* aren't we?" Y asked me. His voice was dry as well. "Any kind of pleasure you can feel in life is selfish. May as well push others aside, devour all the good luck, and find ways to justify yourself after the fact. But once in a while, some guy comes along and messes everything up, as we can see. With all these people in the world, how couldn't there be guys like that? People are disgusting. The number of starving people left to die attests to this. Frankly, with the way things are, I'm impressed that anybody has the nerve to say the world is beautiful, or that they're happy. The fact that anyone can claim they're a good person proves that human beings are monsters. And the more conservative a person is, the angrier they get when you say this kind of thing. What a joke . . . hahaha. Hey, did you notice? I was lying this whole time. I don't believe a word of any of this. I could care less what happens to anybody else."

Y smiled. Bitterly.

"What about the lives of all the people who lived hundreds of thousands of years ago?" he asked. "Who wastes any time thinking of them? I think I said a minute ago that people look like images to me. But it would be more accurate to say that all I see are colors. The colors of their hair, and of their skin, and of their clothes. And all these colors do is move around and talk. Like paint that can stand up and walk around. When you actually think about the way that human beings grow hands, five fingers on each, and walk around picking things up, it's disgusting. The only thing that ever got me going was sex. But even that gets old after a while. What could be worse than where your mind goes right after you jizz? Guys like me, though, who start to tell themselves it can't get much better, imagining how groggy it'll feel in a few seconds, when it's over, we have a hard time even finishing. Know what I mean. Human beings get used to things. That's what we do. Even the freakiest sex act will eventually get boring. That's what happens when imagination and boredom get thrown into the blender . . . Know what your problem is? You can't enjoy your life. You think everybody is below you. Then why should you be here, risking your life like this? I'll tell you why. Force of habit."

Y brought the gun a hair closer to me.

"You've decided that this is your lot in life. You can't enjoy yourself, and you've had plenty of bad luck. But you're weirdly good at what you do, and don't care much about self-preservation, so you wind up saving people all the time. I'm sure you already see yourself and your life this way. With all the people running around out there, almost nobody, on the average day, truly thinks about the shape of their existence or the meaning of their life, but you're all too conscious of the shape your life has taken. That's why you do the things you do. Like you're watching yourself do them . . . but maybe this has gone on long enough? Huh?"

Y took a deep breath and let it all out. Groaning through the exhale.

"It's not like you're attached to anything. You're just like me. A glitch that doesn't make sense, with the world the way it is, but that's somehow gotten this far. Being too clever is a problem too, you know. Right? Just like me, you've got life more or less figured out. So, what happens now? Whose bullet will go where, in each of us? Hm? Know what, though . . . I think I'd like to get off one more time. Ever seen one of these?"

As soon as Y moved his fingers, I pulled the trigger of my gun.

". . . Uh."

It was a dry sound. A sound I'd heard so many times before. Blood was trickling from Y's forehead, as he slowly keeled over. I couldn't feel pain anywhere in my own body.

". . . Whew."

Y muttered something as his body fell. A groan of recognition.

". . . Whoa, whew."

Watching a person die in front of you is a particular experience. It's gotten easier with time, but I can't say that I felt nothing at all. Y's eyes were watching something, oddly focused, but eventually they stopped. Blood was dripping from his mouth. I felt a dire urge to vomit, but I held it back. If there's an afterlife, no matter how I tried to make excuses, I was going straight to hell.

But if I had another chance, I think I'd do it all again. I don't see any other way. I guess this is the life I was supposed to live. If I had let this man survive, harm would have come to Kirita and Yamamoto. I'm not sure what else I could have done. I guess all that was left for me to do was tolerate this feeling, for as long as it lasted.

I was standing there. In a swarm of thoughts. Beside a body, like so many times before.

11

". . . What are you saying?"

"What it sounds like. Y is dead."

Mari Yamamoto was dumbstruck. We were standing by the dirty river alongside her apartment building. The water was mucky. It barely moved.

"All your debts have vanished too, since they were in his name. That means the credit card he gave you won't work anymore either . . . but you can use this."

I handed her a stack of bills that had been scattered over the desk in Y's bedroom. A million and a half. If I'd have left it there, the police would have taken it and put it in the treasury, where it would have barely made a dent.

"Y is . . . dead then?"

"Yeah. That's right."

I looked at Yamamoto. She was crying.

"Now you're free," I said.

There were no birds or fish in the river, which was

basically a drainage easement. Though I could see the front tire of a bicycle. Plastic bottles and tin cans bobbed in the shallows. I wouldn't be surprised if they'd been floating there for years.

"But I'm . . ."

"Past is past. Forget about it."

"Forget it? Easy for you to say. You don't know me. Or what I've been through."

"Quit jabbering." I lit a cigarette.

"At this point, I don't really have a choice . . . right?"

Yamamoto covered her face with her hands and cried. She was all mixed up.

"You need to live your life."

Murky as this river was, as long as no one threw anything else in there, it would clear up over time. The days would go by. I felt my eyes drying out and blinked aggressively.

"As a first step, you should try something new . . . What do you want to try?"

Both sleeves of Yamamoto's shirt were fraying at the wrists. Her hair was cut a little on the short side. If I were to guess, she cut her hair herself.

"Tell me. What do you want to do?"

". . . Paint paintings."

"See, I knew there was something."

"I'm into S&M, and I'd like to keep on doing it . . . but I also think that working as a nurse could be fun, too."

Crying away, Yamamoto crouched down on the sidewalk. The few people out and about turned their heads as they went by. I lit a second cigarette. I was going to keep her company until she was done crying.

It goes without saying, but neither of us knew the other person's entire story. Whenever we meet somebody new, all we pick up about the other person's life is fragments.

I figured this was probably the last time I would see her.

~~~~~~~~~~~~

". . . SOUNDS LIKE the case is closed," said the chief. His office was nonsmoking, but he smoked anyway. "Looks like this guy that we've been calling Y, real name Yutaka Yamada, who murdered Kazunari Yoshikawa, and who murdered Togashi to cover it up, was murdered himself by a gangster, because of money trouble. The guy who did it's on the lam, whereabouts unclear . . . That story sound okay to you?"

"Not to me."

I smiled. The chief made a familiar gesture, telling me to have a smoke.

"I have a carry permit, but there's no mistaking that I shot him in the forehead. He may have been armed, but that's no place for a detective to shoot a man."

"Not to mention the fact . . . that Yutaka Yamada's pistol was empty."

He was right. He had pulled the trigger, but the pistol hadn't fired.

"Of course, you thought that it was loaded. That's why you shot him. Which should be fine. But we know they can be picky about this kind of thing . . . Though I admit, that story isn't worth a damn."

The chief twisted up his lips. It had taken me a while to notice, but he did this all the time.

"Still, this case is a hot potato. Yamada had a robust power base and plenty of allegiances, though some of that has faded over time. Nobody wants to take this one too far. I'm sure there are a handful of crooked politicians who are going to be in trouble without Yamada to protect them, but those guys don't want to make a stink about things. And the first division never seemed to care much this entire time . . . It's the other bad guys, his associates, who came out on the short end of the stick who might come after you. Hence why we don't want the whole world to know the name of the detective that shot the guy. I'll do my best to keep the thing about the bullets under wraps."

". . . Listen, though."

"Hayama. The police withhold the names of people all the time. The fact you shot him will go on the record, obviously, and I'll have to say as much to the higher-ups, but I'll play my cards right to make sure that your name doesn't leak out and wind up in the inbox of the media or any of these shady organizations . . . And I'll make it clear at the top level that if your name does get leaked, a lot of other skeletons are getting pulled out of the closet."

". . . Are you serious?"

"Who do you think I am?"

The chief let out a tired laugh. It made me wish that we had talked a little more.

"I've never done much to distinguish myself on the force, but I made it far as chief, at least of this little police station. I'm good at this kind of thing . . . This is my last big job, before retirement. But there's a chance things won't go so well this time around. If your luck runs out, I'm truly sorry. At that juncture, I'll accept your letter of resignation . . . but if I were you, I'd disappear overseas."

Mikiya Togashi was survived by one family member. Life at home had been rough, and his relationship with his mother was far from rosy. When he was in the fifth grade, she died of a drug overdose, but his father was still alive, living in an old folks' home. Divorced from his second wife, he was suffering from worsening dementia and had moved into the home without informing his son. I saw no need to show up and inform him that his son was dead.

"Here, Togashi's things . . ."

"What am I supposed to do with this?"

We had paid our respects to Togashi at a modest police funeral. His remains had been put into an urn. All that was left was the suit and shoes he had been wearing when he died. Both of which I recognized.

Since Togashi had been inside Yoshikawa's other apartment, there was a chance that he had seen the body. The body by the messy note. If I had found the note in time, we could have made it look like the dead man was responsible for everything, settling the case, at least superficially. I could have saved him.

I should have stopped Togashi when I saw him by the pond. I could have used the element of surprise and detained him. But Togashi was a detective. It may not have gone so well. It may have even ended in a shootout.

Placed neatly between the folded pants and jacket of the suit was a handkerchief. A woman's handkerchief. My heart was beating. It was monogrammed. K.T. As in Kurumi Togashi? That was Togashi's mother's name.

". . . What's up with this handkerchief?"

I was asking the woman from the general affairs department, there beside me. I couldn't get my breath under control.

"I wonder. It's a woman's," she said. "We found it inside of the right pocket of his suit."

Could that mean that when I saw him, he wasn't reaching for a gun, but for this handkerchief? Pawing his way back into childhood? Was he that scared of me, for following him into the woods? Was I really that scary?

". . . I see."

I walked away from her and kept on walking. Unsure of where to go. The door that led out to the fire stairs was just ahead, so I opened it and lit another smoke. Sitting on the top step.

"That guy . . ."

A breeze was blowing. Togashi was long gone, in another world. And I was stuck here.

Just like me, you've got life more or less figured out. At least that's what Y, or Yamada, had said to me.

What was he talking about? My eyes were tearing up. Life. What did I know? What would I ever know?

Epilogue

Maiko Kirita. Real name: Keiko Kirita.

I looked over her record from the children's home she lived in as a girl.

AT AGE SIX, Kirita lost both her parents. They had been less than fortunate. Both of them worked, and from the outside, most would think they were a little too short with their daughter. But in actuality, it was an average home, and Kirita's time with them was uneventful.

She was a pretty girl, selected for the role of Snow White at her preschool's arts festival. The teachers persuaded her parents, who rarely made an appearance on Parents' Day, to take the time off and come by for the performance. They were sore from other parents having told them that they didn't show their child enough love. But it wasn't true that they didn't love their daughter. They were simply busy, and once they had decided to attend the festival, they had looked forward to it, basically. On the walk down to the festival, they were run over by a car and killed. Her mother held on for a few hours, but her father died instantly.

It was a small-town tragedy. Another family was driving over the little bridge down the street when the earthquake hit. It was only magnitude 5.3, with a seismic intensity of under 5, so the earth itself wasn't shaking all that hard, but the decrepit bridge buckled under them and the driver, who was the dad, lost his cool. He stepped on the gas, trying to cross the bridge as quickly as possible. Just before he slammed into the car in front of them, he spun the wheel to the left, in an effort to protect his wife, who was in the passenger seat, and his son, in the back seat behind her, but he ran onto the sidewalk where Kirita's parents were walking. It was a fatal collision, but the bridge did not collapse that day, and the family in the car made a complete recovery, coming away with injuries that healed in a week to a month.

Kirita unreasonably blamed herself. She hadn't even cared if her parents showed up at the festival, but she decided it was all her fault, that she must have given them some kind of look that said she really, really wanted them to come. From then on, she started acting strangely.

The car that ran over her parents was a new model, and at the time, the company was running three different commercials. She taped each of the commercials and watched them over and over again. In each one, a happy family goes shopping or heads off for some adventure in a car just like the one that ran over her parents. When she watched these commercials, young Kirita opened her eyes as wide as they could go. The happy family. Their smiling faces. Happy people.

Obviously, the car wasn't to blame. After all, there was an earthquake. The family wasn't blamed for what happened, either. The adults seemed to recognize that cars were dangerous, and if you got in their way you would die, but this was hard for Kirita, at her age, to accept. The commercials served to absolve this dangerous machine that had run over her parents. Like they were in the right, and she was in the wrong. Kirita was too young to make sense of it, unsure of how to process what had happened. Watching the commercials made her blame herself even more. She slipped into a cramped and agonizing place.

Kirita moved in with relatives, who later passed her off onto another set of relatives, namely a stepfather who became obsessed with the young girl. But he was a cautious man. Before laying a finger on her, he tried to break her spirit.

"It's because you're such a pretty girl that your mother and your father died."

This is how the man retraumatized Kirita, who was eleven at the time. In elementary school.

"It's all your fault. Because you're such a pretty girl.

That's why I feel the way I do. I want to spend all of my time with you, even though I have a wife and son, because you're bad. It's fine, I'm just going to hold your hand. If you tell anyone about this, you'll get thrown out of this house and picked up by kidnappers, or die hungry on the street. I'm not going to force you. It's your decision to make. Want to take a bath with me?"

The adult ego is much stronger than that of the child. Kirita started to bang her arms against her desk on purpose. Not blaming her beauty, so much as blaming her entire self. For everything. She engaged in self-harm as a way of punishing herself. But when her homeroom teacher noticed the bruises on her arms, he felt obligated to speak up. He paid her foster family a visit, but he didn't buy their story about her falling down. Not bothering to wait for the sluggish child welfare office to react, he practically dragged the girl to a psychiatrist.

It's not clear what kind of treatment she received there. But she did stop harming herself. When her foster father threw the TV playing the taped commercials on the floor and finally made a move on her, she bit his hand so hard it took the wound two months to heal.

"This girl was forced to confront the absurdities of the world on her own," says one of the notes left by the psychiatrist who assessed her during her time at the children's home.

It's not clear what happened in her life for a while after

that. The next item in her record was a testimony from a man who was arrested for child prostitution.

They booked the man for picking up Kirita, who by then was seventeen, but the charges had been dropped. He was a math teacher, as well as the advisor for the drama club that Kirita had been a part of. Kirita's body showed the signs of physical restraint, but the man persistently denied having engaged in BDSM or anything of the like. "I'm sure that she had other partners besides me. I think some of them were teachers, too." Or so he testified, but there was no indication of who these other partners might have been.

I met with the teacher who had been arrested. He was working in hospitality, at the ryokan that his parents owned. "Kirita had no romantic feelings for me. I know the way this sounds, coming from someone in my position, but at the time, I was pretty popular among the girls at school . . . She picked me solely for my looks."

He was looking at my cigarette, so I offered him the pack, but he told me he had quit.

"The money that I gave her was supposed to be a kind of an allowance. She was the one who pursued me and initiated sex. When one of the other teachers found out, all the girls went nuts with jealousy and got the police involved . . . The case was thrown out, but I had to give up teaching. Odd as it may sound, though, I don't really regret it."

The man kept giving me this feeble sort of smile. He had seen better days, but he had a handsome nose and could have been a hunky guy once upon a time.

"She had a history of being bullied. A lot of other awful things had happened to her in her life. Sometimes I wondered if she wasn't in the drama club because she wanted to be someone else . . . One time, she told me something strange. That whenever something bad happened, she touched herself. She meant . . . touching herself sexually. Said it was because that part of her was hidden, a secret place that no one knew. Hers and hers alone . . . She said that she could take all of the pain the world had given her and change it into pleasure. Same went for masturbation and for sex. She said it made the bad things disappear. And that S&M turned everything upside down, like it was flipped . . . She used me like a tool. Though in her case, it'd be fair to say that every man she's ever been with was a tool to her."

Kirita, however, did not start working as a sex worker. Leaving the theater behind, she moved to Tokyo and found a job as a hostess at a club, practicing BDSM as a hobby on the side. Which is when she caught the attention of the chairman of a company with an unpleasant reputation.

I asked Kaminuma what he knew. At first he stalled, insisting it was only hearsay, but eventually he talked.

"From the sounds of it, the chairman was a pushy guy

and wound up assaulting her. Helping himself to the sex that had been her refuge . . . But that's how she met Y."

When the chairman tried assaulting her again, Kirita stabbed him. Consumed by fear, she called the manager of the club where she was working, and the manager showed up with Y. Y gave the dead man a careful once-over and said something obtuse, about how people who get stabbed to death usually look more surprised, then turned to Kirita and said, "You need another story."

The way she stabbed him, it was going to be hard to get away with self-defense. Y wasn't talking about jail, though, but about taking on another story. Kirita had her fingerprints erased and changed the way she looked. She started carrying a counterfeit ID that said her name was Maiko. This wasn't about changing who she was, so much as how she was.

Y assured her that nobody, man or woman, can be stained by sex. Biologically speaking, he explained, human beings are made of elementary particles, and that by intaking nutrients and excreting waste, we replace all of the cells in our entire body every year. That even if she was filmed doing whatever, it's really just a digitized signal being reproduced by a device, fundamentally no more than a sophisticated picture, so it wasn't actually the case that anyone was watching her go at it. That even if a gross man forced himself upon her and made her feel things, she had absolutely no reason to blame herself. And that while some men may yammer on about what makes the female body beautiful, it's possible for a gross woman to make a man ejaculate against his will, if she ties him up and stimulates him properly. Biological mechanics. That's all there was to human beings.

"Rape and sex are completely different things. Don't let it get to you. Men like him are scum. Just let it go. Stick with me and you'll be fine."

Kirita became Y's woman. But his personality was already disintegrating.

That was all that I had been able to find out about Kirita.

"Something odd about her," Kaminuma told me, in conclusion. "Since she was six, she's never once been in a car. In today's world, can you imagine? I love driving. Hey, you've got a Benz, so you must love driving too. But she wouldn't even go on her school trips, because they used a bus . . . She rides the train no problem, though, which is sort of hypocritical . . . It's gotta be tough, living that way. It's like part of her is stuck, like she's still six years old."

LEANING AGAINST THE wall outside Kirita's apartment building, I snuffed out my cigarette in my portable ashtray. Kirita blew past me, rolling a purple suitcase.

"Where to?" I asked.

She spun around, but she didn't look surprised. Smiled

at me, rather innocently. Seems like she had noticed I was there already. She sure was beautiful. I had never seen a face so beautiful or, better put, a face that stung my heart with such dizzying precision.

"I suppose that I have you to thank for emptying out Y . . . Yamada's gun."

People were walking past us on the sidewalk. Heading both directions.

"I thought that you weren't interested in me, but you're persistent . . . You're a funny detective."

"Tell me."

Kirita didn't say a thing.

"You did it because you didn't want Yamada killing anybody else . . . If it wasn't for this simplistic whim of yours, I probably would have died. How did you know that I would find him?"

But Kirita only smiled.

"New question." I took a deep breath. "What made you kill Yoshikawa?"

Kirita's eyebrows twitched. I tried again to even out my breathing.

"I know it wasn't Yamada that killed Yoshikawa. It was you. You used that bronze bird glazed with white enamel. You did a sloppy job of cleaning up the fingerprints and bloodstains, but blood can't be wiped up so easily. If you sprinkle murder weapons with a special chemical, any trace of blood will cause what's called a luminol reaction.

The blood streaks only showed up faintly, but there was something odd about the pattern. It never would have looked this way unless the murderer had held the bird in their right hand, with all five fingers. I'm sure of it. Five fingers, dripping blood. You could see it in the pattern of the streaks."

I stood there, somehow unable to move any closer to her.

"Yoshikawa's body showed no signs of having been tied up. Which means he wasn't tied up when you killed him. If you'd wanted to kill him, you could have done it easily any of the times that you had him restrained. But since you didn't, it must have been self-defense. Right? Yoshikawa went nuts. He tried to kill himself and take you with him. We know he didn't die immediately. His knees were bent too much for someone who had fallen. After you hit him the first time, he must have gotten on his knees. To express his gratitude. Then he begged you to hit him once more with the bird, which you did, knocking him over . . . In short, he assaulted you because he wanted you to kill him. That's how it looks to me."

"That bird statue," Kirita said. Not smiling anymore. She stared directly at me. "At first, when he untied me, he was careful with me, he was gentle. But he transformed out of nowhere . . . He went to put his hands around my neck. I tried to run away, but then he caught up with me . . . *Look*, he said. Pointing at the bird statue. *Look,*

look . . . Before I knew it, I had hit him in the head . . . After that, it's like you just described. Yoshikawa got on his knees, really dizzy, and said to do it again. In a pleading voice. I should have called an ambulance. But I guess I got sucked into the pleading expression on his face . . . so I hit him again. Sometimes I get the scary feeling that he's still alive somewhere, and that he's going to come by and beg to do it again . . . When it happened, the blood was so incredible, so, so much blood, all the life coming out of him. Even still, though."

"Let me guess—*poor thing*?"

Kirita was silent.

". . . There's just one thing I'd like you to explain. Why would you help Yamada kill Togashi? I know you helped him. But why do it?"

"It started when he told me to seduce him, but things went too far, so I broke things off."

Kirita continued. Gazing straight into my eyes.

"But not long after I killed Yoshikawa, Togashi rang my doorbell. Yamada was actually over at the time . . . He had been eating pills like candy, so he was pretty high. He said something about how he had predicted this would happen and started scribbling in his planner. Then he grabbed his shoes and hid out on the balcony. I told Togashi exactly what Yamada told me to say. I messed it up a little towards the end, accidentally telling him the truth, or part of it. I gave him the planner, though . . . but after that, Yamada told me to seduce Togashi again, and this time film it. He said that if I didn't, he'd kill Togashi. I couldn't tell if Yamada wanted to keep me under his thumb, or wanted to destroy me. I did it with Togashi, so that Yamada could watch . . . but Yamada got anxious, and said he was going to kill Togashi anyway. I was like, that's not what you promised me. But when I tried to stop him, he said okay, how about I die instead, and held a pistol to his temple, laughing the whole time . . . Yamada was ready to die. When he got excited like that, he always followed through on what he said. That's who he was. But I chose him over Togashi. That's why I did it."

"Did what?"

"Before Yamada killed Togashi, I wanted to make love to him, just one more time . . . Togashi had been chasing me forever. I know this was beside the point, but still."

Togashi had problems. One being a desire to redeem his mother, who had been cast out of society, and make her happy. The other being a desire to become one with the men who slept with her and sleep with her himself. When Togashi tried to help Kirita get away, and when he slept with her, he was exercising the two contradictory forces at the center of his life. Togashi's shoes, the two of them, appeared before me. I wondered whether he and Kirita used ropes. Ropes to tether someone down who was about to vanish.

". . . I couldn't blame Togashi . . . and if he hadn't

covered for me at the start, I would have been arrested
. . . He was a nice guy. But faced with a choice between
Yamada killing himself and Togashi dying, I got con-
fused . . ."

"Why would you confess like this, so easily?"

"That's what you wanted, isn't it?"

Togashi had met his ruin. But he gave it his best effort,
the way I see it, anyway. I'm not so sure about Yamada, but
I think that Yoshikawa and Kirita gave it their best efforts,
too. Not in terms of good or bad, but considering the
forms of their existences. This was simply the result of all
the different lines—all of the fragments of their respec-
tive lives—getting tangled up in one big knot.

I supposed that it's the same for me. I've killed my share
of people in my day. I'll never get over Kyoko. I'll continue
going to that bar I like and ordering the croque monsieur,
which isn't on the menu. I get depressed, unable to fix
things, and I'm resigned to being disappointed with the
world. But that's me doing my best. I will keep on living
life this way, until I die for one reason or another.

Kirita stared at me. The breeze coiled around us. My
eyes were dry again. I blinked.

". . . The first time you came by my apartment, you
turned me down. If you had done it with me then, I think
I would have told you everything there was to know about
Yamada . . . That's how it felt to me, at the time. But you
turned me down . . . My whole life, I've never really liked

someone before. Of course I've felt desire, or felt sorry for people, or wanted to be with them, but I don't know, this feels different . . . Maybe I'm mistaken, though."

Some of Kirita's bangs were sticking to her forehead. Before one of us could comb them back, the breeze took care of it. I took a breath, making sure she didn't catch on.

". . . You're mistaken."

For a second, Kirita looked distraught, but soon enough she looked at me and laughed.

". . . Such a lonely man."

She bobbed her head, nodding at me, then walked off smiling. Not in heels, but sneakers.

Kirita was arguably a danger to society. As I watched her walk away, that crossed my mind. Were she to get involved with the wrong person again, there might be another incident. But I wasn't about to try and stop her. I suppose there was a chance that we might get entangled in each other's lives again. Now and then, something flashes at us from the desert of reality. Years go by between these moments. Even so, I couldn't bring myself to stop her.

I watched Kirita slip away. I couldn't claim to know that much about her.

—*You sure? She's getting away.*

Was that Kyoko's voice? I smiled ruefully. Because I was tired. I hadn't had a good night's sleep in I don't know how long.

"It's fine. I can't arrest her."

—*That's not what I meant.*

". . . I'm fine with you being the last woman I'm ever with."

Kirita crossed through the shadows cast in the road by the telephone poles. Unlike the others who had vanished, she was heading towards reality. When she reached the road ahead of us, with all the people going by, she would blend into the crowd. But I just stood there, watching her back. She slipped away. I lit a cigarette.

—*Are you sure you're fine?*

I blinked. Once, twice. She was disappearing. On the road ahead.

Selected Bibliography and DVDs

新版 古事記 現代語訳付き [Kojiki: A New Edition with a Modern Translation]. Trans. Hirotoshi Nakamura. Kadokawa Sophia Bunko. ISBN: 4044001049

日本書紀 全現代語訳（上、下）[Nihonshoki: A Complete Modern Translation (Two Volumes)]. Trans. Tsutomu Ujitani. Kodansha Gakujutsu Bunko. ISBN: 4061588338 (Vol. 1), 4061588346 (Vol. 2)

国家神道と日本人 [State Shinto and the Japanese]. Susumu Shimazono. Iwanami Shinsho. ISBN: 4004312590

アマテラスの誕生―古代王権の源流を探る [The Birth of Amaterasu—Seeking the Sources of Ancient Royalty]. Mutsuko Mizoguchi. Iwanami Shinsho. ISBN: 4004311713

日本神話の源流 [Sources of Japanese Mythology]. Atsuhiko Yoshida. Kodansha Gakujutsu Bunko. ISBN: 4061598201

大麻と古代日本の神々 [Cannabis and the Kami of Ancient Japan]. Hiroshi Yamaguchi. Takarajimasha Shinsho. ISBN: 480022456X

サピエンス全史 文明の構造と人類の幸福（上、下） [Sapiens: A Brief History of Humankind (Two Volumes)]. Yuval Noah Harari. Trans. Yasushi Shibata. Kawade Shobo Shinsha. ISBN: 430922671X (Vol. 1), 4309226728 (Vol. 2)

緊縛の文化史 [The Beauty of Kinbaku]. Master "K." Trans. Norio Yamamoto. Suirensha. ISBN: 4863692994

縛師—Bakushi [Kinbaku Master]. DVD. Dir. Ryuichi Hiroki. Geneon Entertainment Inc.

雪村春樹の縛り方講座〜情愛縛りで楽しむ〜 [Haruki Yukimura's Shibari Course—Enjoying Affectionate Shibari]. DVD. Van Associates.

縄遊戯　雪村流縛り方講座 永久保存版 [Rope Play: The Yukimura Shibari Course—Collector's Edition]. DVD. Van Associates.

生物と無生物のあいだ [Between Animate and Inanimate]. Shinichi Fukuoka. Kodansha Gendai Shinsho. ISBN: 4061498916

Afterword to the Japanese Paperback Edition

This novel is my nineteenth book to date.

A literary work, it has some deviant noir elements, as well as a hardboiled feel. As I mentioned in my afterword to the Japanese hardcover, what I was hoping to convey was this sense of a dim light through a veil of fog, in which the fragments of a few lives overlap, to form a story. Without incorporating methods from several different genres, I never could have brought this novel into being.

Reading it again after some time, I'm struck by how firmly it prods at the most delicate parts of me. The same applies to all my works, but this one especially. Of all the books that I've written over the years, this novel has a special place in my heart.

I'm deeply thankful to "R" for answering my questions about kinbaku and BDSM and for being a huge source of inspiration to this work. Without her help, I never would have been able to write the book that you see here.

In technical terms, when I say deviantly noir, I'm talking about how making Togashi narrate the first half of the book, which under normal circumstances would have been a procedural narrated by Hayama, allows for the investigation to proceed behind his back—alienating Togashi from what seems like his own story. This sense of alienation was essential to fleshing out his character. So that his character was defined not only by description, but through the structure as well.

I also paid attention to the colors used for characters. Maiko's sweats are purple, a color that has sensual connotations, but she's first described wearing a beige cardigan, more of an ambiguous color, which she uses to conceal herself. While none of the female characters is better than the others, Y has his own preferences, and uses something like the Twelve Level Cap and Rank System of the Asuka period (purple to blue, in descending order) to color code the women under his control.

These observations may come across as superfluous, but as it's been about three years since the hardcover came out, it's my hope that you will kindly accept them as the casual remarks of an author peering into the machinery of his writing after some time away. This is generally a job best left to literary critics, but since nobody has pointed these things out, I figured why not. Though there have been plenty of fine observations.

As of 2022, I will have been working as an author for twenty years. It's thanks to you, my readers, that I've made it this far. I'm sincerely thankful for your continued support. Living can be sad sometimes, but I hope that you'll continue to keep me company in the life ahead.

See you next time.

6 July 2021
Fuminori Nakamura

(Author's Note: The origins of kinbaku, including torinawajutsu and other methods for tying people up, extend much further back than the Edo period, but I have followed precedent and used this timeframe as a starting point, since this is when the basic forms that we call kinbaku today took shape. As for the passage on page 224 about Shinto teachings, shrines do often stage ritual acts of purification called harae, as is widely known.)